Thomasine

Queensland Pioneer
Nerang River & Gold Coast

Sandra J. Darroch

The Svengali Press

2, 2-4 Notts Ave
Bondi Beach NSW 2026
AUSTRALIA

trilby@svengalipress.com.a
u
www.svengalipress.com.au

Digital editions in association with ETT Imprint, Exile Bay

ISBN 978-0-6489227-1-1 (paper)
ISBN 978-1-922473-43-1 (ebook)

Cover painting of Thomasine by Paul Delprat.

CONTENTS

OTHER BOOKS BY
THIS AUTHOR

Titles marked with * are available as e-books and Print-on-Demand (POD worldwide.

ONCE UPON A VASE (Macmillan Aust.)

*OTTOLINE: THE LIFE OF LADY OTTOLINE MORRELL (Chatto & Windus UK); Coward McCann & Geoghegan (USA) 1975-76

BLOKES (Pan Books) Sydney and London,1984.

*POWER FOR THE PEOPLE (Svengali Press Aust., UK. USA) 2015

*GARSINGTON REVISITED (Svengali Press, Aust., UK, USA) 2017

*AFTER THE ULTIMATE VIRUS (Svengali Press Aust, UK. USA) 2020

The Svengali Press publishes good books which the big publishers overlook. Our list can be viewed at: www.svengalipress.com.au

If you have an unpublished manuscript ready for publication, please contact us for assessment at: trilby@svengalipress.com.au

Thomasine Browne

INTRODUCTION

THOMASINE BROWNE was a brave and intrepid individual. Undeterred by the shocking news of the murder of her father and brother in New Zealand by the Maoris when she was a young mother and widow, Thomasine gave up a privileged future in London to sail up the isolated Nerang River through bush-jungle wilderness in Southern Queensland in 1864 with her second husband, Walter John Browne. (Walter is referred to as "Jack" in this book because that was his name to Thomasine, the family, and their friends).

Thomasine and Jack and her four young children from her first marriage to Rev. Edward James Cooper, lived in a totally isolated tent in the bush-jungle for two years before they built and moved into their first house. They had ten more children together, seven of whom survived, bringing her total surviving family to 11 children. She established not only the first European family on the Nerang, but also helped to build the Nerang community, and encouraged the development of the Arts and Music. I am proud to be one of Thomasine's great-great- granddaughters.

A bridge spanning the highway leading into Nerang is named the "Walter J. Browne" bridge, celebrating the foresight and pioneering spirit of Jack, my great-great grandfather, who did so much to create and build the community of the Nerang area which later developed into the Gold Coast. A book dedicated to his pioneering work also needs to be written.

No bridge celebrates Thomasine, but I hope this book will act as a small tribute to her courage and enthusiasm for her new country.

This book is what I call a "docu-novel," or a "bio-novel," being a re-creation of Thomasine and her world, based on my research into documented historical facts and family lore, but "brought to life" by the technique of the novelist.

– Sandra J. Darroch

DEDICATION

To my cousin, Genevieve Grainger, a dedicated, expert genealogist, and researcher, who gave me invaluable help and support during the research and writing of this book.

ACKNOWLEDGEMENTS

With great thanks to the following people without whose help this book couldn't have been written: my first cousin, Genevieve Grainger, whose research skills have been invaluable to me in writing this book; family historian and archivist, Sue (Cooper) Mills*, a descendant of Thomasine's first marriage to Rev. Edward James Cooper, has provided family photographs and documents, plus local knowledge, all of which has been a great help to me; my brother, Richard Jobson, who has also provided very useful family material, and who took me on a guided tour of the Nerang; Jack Rudd, another descendant of Thomasine, who gave me information about Walter John "Jack" Browne's military activities; thanks, too, to The City of Gold Coast Library; The Local Studies Library, Southport; The Gold Coast Hinterland Heritage Museum Inc.; and a particular tribute to Robert Longhurst for his invaluable book, *Nerang Shire a History to 1949*. (Queensland, The Albert Shire Council, 1994): and thanks to the authors of all the books, manuscripts and other documents listed in the Bibliography at the end of this book; thanks, too, to Peter Jeffery for his technical assistance in producing this book

*Note: Letters from Thomasine and other family members quoted in this book are courtesy Sue Mills. I have substituted a stock font for reproducing Thomasine's letters because although she had good handwriting, (see example below) her letters have been damaged by age, making the original handwriting difficult to decipher in parts.

1

Dire News

ON A SOFT late September afternoon in 1863 Walter "Jack" Browne, a tall young man with a military bearing, yet wearing lavender-coloured kid gloves, stands at the front door of an elegant townhouse in London's Bayswater. A maid answers the door and Jack explains:

"Sir William Keith Ball has asked me to deliver a letter to Mrs Thomasine Cooper. May I please come in?"

The maid takes his top hat, coat and kid gloves and ushers him down the hallway towards the drawing room.

As he walks down the darkened hallway, Jack can hear the strains of a piano melody – Schubert – and he recalls that Thomasine had always been a talented pianist. *It must be seven years since I've seen Thomasine,* Jack muses, recalling the young woman who had confided her witty and penetrating observations of their extended family clan at gatherings in the little Hereford village of Stoke Prior. Although Thomasine is four years older than him, she has always treated him as an equal. How would she be now, a widow at 29, and mother of four young children – and about to learn from him some dreadful news?

Jack pauses in the drawing room doorway for a moment, taking in the sight of a dark-haired, slender woman sitting at a piano, shafts of autumn sunlight catching auburn tints in her hair. A vase of fresh deep blue irises on the piano brightens up the otherwise dark Victorian furnishings of the room.

"Jack!" exclaims Thomasine, looking up, surprised at seeing him after all these years.

"Tommy!" replies Jack, bounding towards her and holding out his hands.

"It's lovely to see you after all this time!" Thomasine says, rising from the piano stool and leading him to a brown velvet sofa under the window.

"Now tell me what you've been up to all these years."

Jack hesitates, knowing that the envelope he carries, addressed to her from her brother Henry in New Zealand, contains dire information. But he decides it is better to indulge in some polite conversation for a moment or two.

"Well, Tommy," he begins, "Since I last saw you at your grandparents' house in Stoke Prior, I've been away in India with the British Army. I finished school at the age of 16 and naively set off to fight in the Indian Mutiny, but alas, when I finally got there, the Mutiny had been quelled and the country was now under the mantle of the British Raj. I stayed on, serving in the British Army, until my parents paid me out, and now I'm here. I would have contacted you earlier, but I'd heard you were married and living in Yorkshire.

"It's only lately that I heard you had become engaged[1] to "Uncle" Keith (as he calls Sir William Keith Ball), following the sad death of your husband. But that's enough catching up for the moment…I'm afraid I've come bearing bad news."

"Oh?" inquires Thomasine, looking at Jack in surprise. "What kind of bad news?"

Jack takes the envelope out of his pocket, explaining that ' "Uncle" Keith had asked him to bring it to her because, he, "Uncle" Keith, had a hansom cab waiting in the street outside his house in Leinster Gardens, Bayswater, opposite Hyde Park, ready to take him to catch the overnight train to Aberdeen on urgent family business. As he waited in the hallway for the cab, Keith had spied two letters on the silver platter on the hall table. Opening the one addressed to him and quickly reading it, he realised the importance of the contents of the other letter, addressed to "Mrs Thomasine Cooper", and so had asked Jack, who happened to be staying with him, to take the letter, *poste haste*, to Thomasine.

Thomasine opens the letter and begins to read it. The address at the top of the notepaper is Cuba Street, Wellington, New Zealand, dated July 7th 1863. The letter has taken over two months to reach her.

"Oh! It's from my brother Henry," she observes. "I haven't heard from him since he married Louisa. She and I didn't get on, for some reason."

She reads on. The letter begins: "My Dearest Sister Thomasine,

"I have the most terrible and tragic news to impart to you.

"Our Dearest Father, Michael, and our Dearest Brother, Frederick, have been brutally murdered as they went about their daily labour on their farm outside Auckland, axed to death, by savage Maoris." The letter goes on to give further details of the shock of the event for their mother, and the reaction to it by the other British settlers in New Zealand.

"I'm sure this dreadful event will reach the British newspapers soon," Henry goes on. "We don't have international telegraph facilities here in New Zealand yet."

"Every attempt is being made to track down the culprits – said to be four young Maori tribesmen. But the murder has set alight a tinderbox of trouble and I suspect we're in for an almighty Maori war. Trouble between the Maori and the British settlers has been brewing for a long time." He added that their mother, Eliza, and the youngest of her nine surviving children, Rowland Joseph, aged 12, and Louisa Rosamond, seven, were being cared for by neighbours, a coroner's inquest was to be held, and the government of New Zealand was bound, eventually, to provide Eliza and her children with a pension to help compensate for her loss.[2]

"I just wish I had never persuaded Father to come out here to New Zealand. I feel it's all my fault," Henry concludes, signing the letter "Your Loving Brother, Henry."

On reading this shattering news, Thomasine sits perfectly still, her face white. Then she begins to sob wildly. Jack leans over and puts his arm around her shoulder.

"Oh, Tommy, Tommy, I'm so sorry," he says, attempting to calm her violent weeping.

"My poor, poor father," sobs Thomasine. "We all thought that at long last some good luck had come his way. He had always suffered a trying existence and worked so hard to bring up his family. He sounded so happy in his last letter to me, describing how he and Eliza and the children had built a little wooden house on their allotment outside the town of Auckland on the North Island and were settling into farm life in New

Zealand – a new country, a new start in life – even though he was getting on in years – he was 59.

"My father never spoke about his troubles and never boasted of what his father had been. He was an honourable and religious man and industrious."[3]

Jack feels helpless, unable to calm Thomasine's tears. They sit together silently on the sofa for a long moment, only interrupted by Nora, the maid, coming in to light the lamps and to announce that Nanny has bathed the younger children and they were now ready for supper upstairs.

Thomasine and Jack stand up.

"Thank you, Nora," Thomasine says. "I'll be up in a few minutes after I've seen Mr Browne to the door."

Turning to Jack, she thanks him for coming. "I shan't ever cry a single tear again," she vows. And she is to keep that vow for the rest of her life.

"I hope we'll see one another again when I've recovered from this dreadful news," she says. And indeed, they are to meet one another again soon – as we shall see later.

Jack bids farewell and returns to Leinster Gardens, drained by the emotions of that afternoon visit, and Thomasine slowly climbs the stairs to the nursery. As she sits down at the nursery supper table with her four children, holding hands to say grace, she does not realise that the events of that day will change the entire direction of her life.[4]

END NOTES CHAPTER 1

[1] Browne, Lyn, *The Two Families of Thomasine Browne.* (1941). Unpublished manuscript, courtesy Sue Mills. (This book has been published in New Zealand under the title *The Two Families of Thomasine Meredith* – available in the Alexander Turnbull Library in the National Library of New Zealand, Wellington.

[2] *The Meredith and Others Pension Act, 1870,* Queen Victoria, New Zealand Government

[3] Thomasine quoted in *The Two Families of Thomasine Browne*, ibid.

Dire News

[4] Waveney Browne stated in *Letters to Bundall* (Local Studies Library, Southport).p. 245: *At the time when Sir William Ball was paying court to Mrs Cooper, Sir William received news that Mrs Cooper's father and brother had been massacred by the Maoris at the outbreak of the Maori War in New Zealand. He was unable to break the news himself and asked Captain Browne to do so.*

2

Thomasine's Father,
Michael Meredith

NEXT MORNING Thomasine wakes up and goes to her bedroom window and looks down at the grey Autumn morning. Her mind feels as dead as the dry leaves swirling around the street below; she simply can't bring herself to think about the terrible news of the murders of her father and brother. She goes about her morning routine, getting the children up and breakfasted with Nanny's help, and dressing them in warm coats for a walk in Kensington Gardens.

Sitting on a park bench watching the children running through the trees, Thomasine finally finds herself grappling with the dire news, images of her father darting into her mind's eye, memories of his steel-grey eyes and black hair, his warm smile and his strong arms when he helped her onto her pony as a child.

What a tragic life that dear man has had. Such a good man, he tried so hard, but Fate was against him, she thinks, as more and more memories flood through her mind...

****

Indeed, Thomasine's father, Michael Meredith, had not been blessed by Fate. He had grown up at *The Heath*, a large manor house in Herefordshire, not far from the village of Stoke Prior where his family, originally from Wales, had settled several generations ago. The second son of the lord of the manor, young Michael had a miserable upbringing. His father, Michael Meredith Snr. was the illegitimate son of a wealthy Herefordshire landowner, Richard Edwards, and his housekeeper, Ann Meredith. On his death in 1774, Richard Edwards' Will[1] had left the bulk of his estates in several parishes

The first page of Richard Edwards' four-page Will

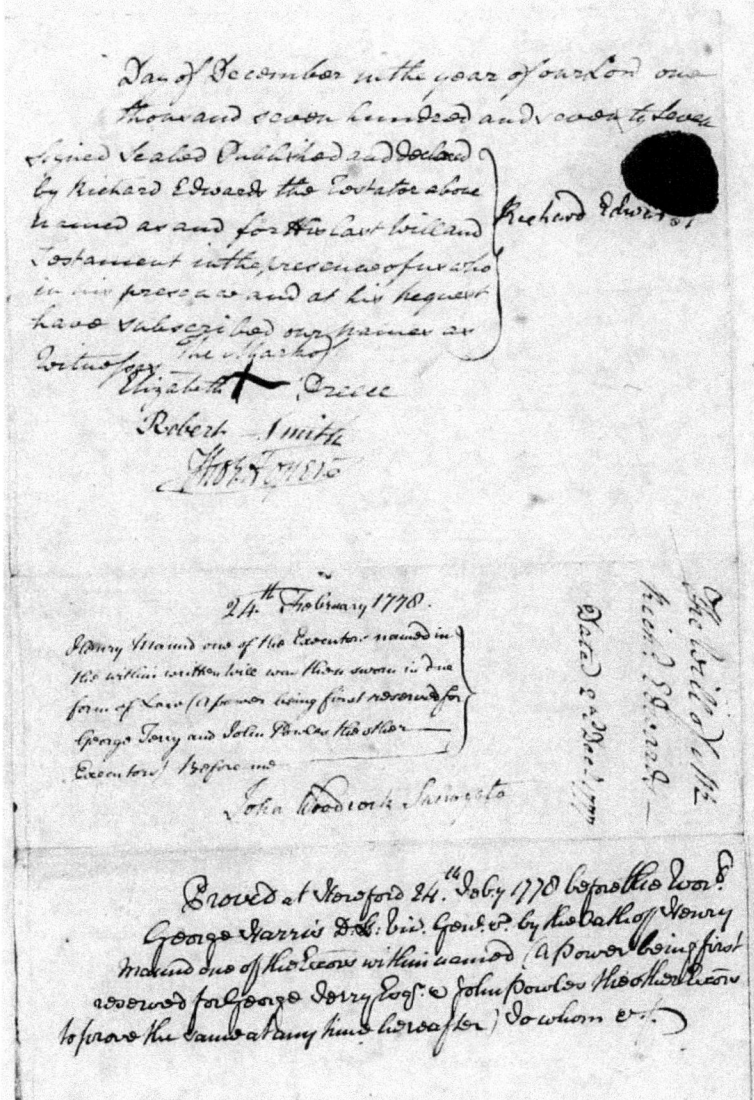

Final page of Richard Edwards' Will

such as Stoke Prior, Humber and Risbury, to his young son, Michael, then aged four, with instructions that he be properly educated and looked after until he reached the legal age of adulthood when he turned 21.[2]

After coming of age, Michael (Snr.) married Molina Greenwood[3], the daughter of another local landowner, who had expected she would continue to live in comfort for the rest of her life on her husband's estates, with income from apple and pear orchards, cider-making, Hereford cattle, and forest timber. her husband was an important man, High Constable of the County, and her parents believed she had married well. But, alas, he turned to drink, and by the age of 30 was consuming a bottle of port before lunchtime each day. He neglected his farming properties and lost large sums of money, gambling, until the estate was in ruins. His second son, Michael [Thomasine's father], had, at the age of 15, taken over the role of Master for Hounds of his father's pack, and devoted himself to tending the horses, suffering repeated beatings by his drunken father, and subject to bullying in the manor stables by his older brother, Richard[4], and the estate's steward, Mortimer, whose avaricious eyes were focused on taking over the estate. Mortimer regarded young Michael as a potential threat to his plans. [5]

By the age of 16 in 1819, young Michael had had enough. Due to bad debts, his father had, the previous year, agreed to sell *The Heath* to a local up-and-coming landowner, John Arkwright, who was busily purchasing a lot of property in the area, and Michael's family were in the process of moving out. Michael packed his bags, farewelled his mother and his father, who somewhat fatuously vowed to cut hm out of his Will – there being virtually nothing of any worth left to bestow on a son. Then Michael walked out onto the old Roman road leading to the hamlet of Stoke Prior where he knocked on the door of a sturdy house, the residence of James Preece, a wealthy timber merchant, and his wife, Ann. Mrs Preece welcomed Michael in and he explained that he was off to London to seek his fortune and wanted to say goodbye to their young daughter, Eliza, aged eight, whom he had taught to ride. He had grown fond of Eliza, a tall girl for her age, with green eyes and dark curls. She had shown an aptitude for riding and he promised to return as soon as he could and would take her for a ride over the downs.

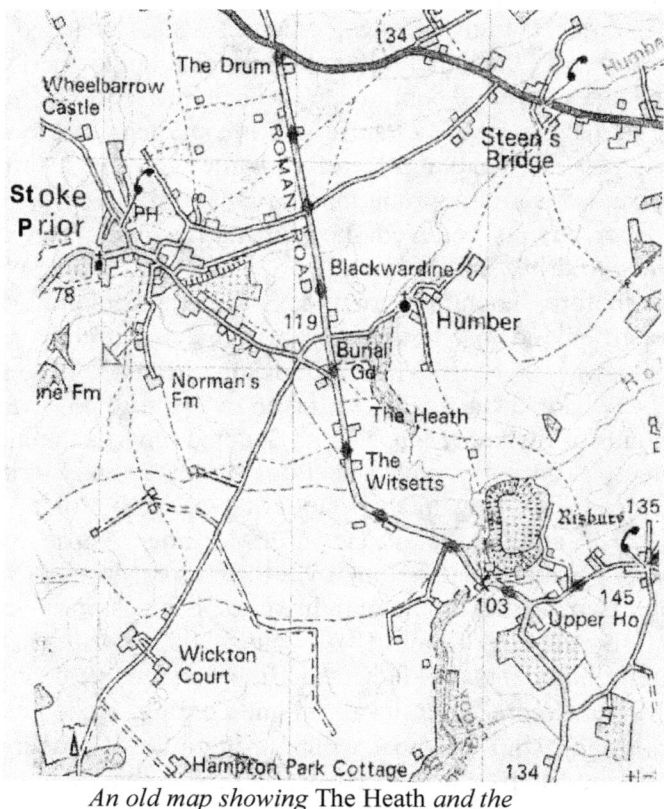

An old map showing The Heath *and the route Michael took to Stoke Prior*

Michael then walked on to the big town of Leominster, about two-and-a-half miles (4km) from Stoke Prior, where he caught the coach to London. The journey took several days to reach the great metropolis.

London in 1819, was buzzing. It was the year Queen Victoria was born, and Michael found himself in a fast-expanding city of over two million people, poised for massive building works during the Victorian age and when it was superseded by the Georgian age. The city was already overcrowded, and its poorer inhabitants endured stark conditions, their health suffering the ever-more-dense fogs caused by coal smoke mixing with the natural Thames Valley fogs to create what is today called "smog". Michael managed to find cheap lodgings in Soho, the closest inexpensive area to Mayfair and Park Lane, where he hoped to find work in the stables of one of the great houses. After a long week applying to the stable managers there, he finally found work in the stables of a duke's daughter, whose husband was a Member of Parliament.

As Michael helped her up onto her mount on his first day of work in the stables, his new employer was surprised to hear his relatively cultivated accent – unlike that of the other grooms' Cockney tones – and, admiring his handsome face, she decided he should be outfitted in smart livery and allotted the task of looking after her young daughter on her daily rides on her Shetland pony on Rotten Row. The remainder of each day was spent exercising the other horses and mucking out the stable, but Michael enjoyed these daily excursions to the fashionable riding and carriage track that stretched from Hyde Park Corner down to the Serpentine. It had been created by William III at the turn of the 17th century as a short cut to St James's Palace and had started out being called *Route de Roi*, but by the time Michael was working there, this name had long since been corrupted to Rotten Row.

Each year, over the next ten years, Michael saved sufficient money for a trip back to the village of Stoke Prior to visit the Preeces and young Eliza, who was growing up to be a clever young woman, good at arithmetic. Her father had bemoaned the fact that she was a girl. "If she'd been a boy she could have taken over the business," he said.

Michael didn't bother to visit the remnants of his own family. His mother had died of a heart attack (or was it a broken heart?) on May 31st 1819, soon after he had left home, and he certainly had no desire to see his father[6] or elder brothers again, and his younger brother had died.

By the time Eliza was 18 and Michael 26, they walked out together publicly whenever he came back to Stoke Prior, and everybody regarded them as a couple. It didn't matter to the village that Michael was no longer "the rich boy from *The*

Heath" and was now working as a lowly stable groom in London. He was family, and Stoke Prior families stuck together.

In 1829 on one of his visits, Michael proposed to Eliza and she accepted. She had been wooed by other young men in the village, but she had only ever had one young man in her mind; Michael. Two years later, in November 1831, their wedding (paid for of course by Eliza's father), took place at the rather grand Christopher Wren-designed St James church in Piccadilly, witnessed by Eliza's brother, William, and her cousin, Thomasine Preece, who was around Eliza's age, and whose name Eliza was to borrow for her first child.

St James church Piccadilly

Married life for the young couple, despite their cramped quarters and the need to share a frugal supply of putrid sewage-filled, Thames water with the other inhabitants of their Soho slum building, was happy until Eliza gave birth to her first baby, christened Thomasine. Living in their cramped rooms with a young baby was soon intolerable, and Michael then rented a small rundown two-up, two-down terrace cottage in Paddington for £14[7] a year, and managed to find a new job as a lowly porter at the recently-built Paddington railway station, starting on a wage of 17/6 a week, moving up to 18/-. Working there was a complete change from the stables, and Michael soon found himself as a small cog in the growing Industrial Revolution in Britain. He had become infected with a touch of the "Railway Mania" which was sweeping the country as investors developed a growing enthusiasm for the huge iron horses snorting steam as they roared out of the countryside into the London terminuses along the many new railway lines established by private companies in the heat of "Railway Mania". [8]

Next, in 1835, Michael and Eliza's son, Henry, was born – the second of the 11 children Eliza and Michael were to have (nine of whom survived). Meanwhile, young Thomasine, now nearly two, was causing her parents concern. She was perennially coughing and suffering bronchitis. Eliza began to feel overwhelmed trying to cope with the newly-born Henry and a sick toddler. By the time Thomasine was three, Eliza had twins on May 11th 1836, (William and James). The little two-up, two-down was becoming decidedly crowded, and by early 1837 Eliza and Michael made a big decision: young Thomasine should go to live with her grandparents at Stoke Prior until the fresh air and country food restored her to health. Indeed, Thomasine soon recovered her health and spent the next four years until she was seven out in the fields in summertime, roaming around with the local children, picking blackberries and splashing in the river.

All this while Michael had continued working as a railway porter at Paddington and later at Aldbury, his stubborn nature providing him with the grit to put up with the harsh working conditions which beat many other railway workers at that time (staff turnover in the railways was extremely high). With a growing family to feed, what else could he do? But he heard that the first inter-city railway line, the London and Birmingham Railway, was opening up along much of the route of the old Grand Union Canal from the newly-built Euston Station[9] in London in 1837, (the year Queen Victoria ascended the throne of Great Britain and Ireland), with a series of smaller stations along its route to Birmingham. Michael saw his chance to gain promotion, earn more, and move his family out of London to the countryside. He decided initially to apply for a job at Euston station in 1838 and gained employment once again as a porter, but at a slightly increased wage of £1 a week.

The first station out of London from Euston was at Tring, 30-odd miles north-west of London. (The train service had begun on October 16th 1837, leaving Primrose Hill at 9am arriving at Tring at 10.10am.) and Michael vowed to demonstrate he was a good employee at Euston and then apply for work at Tring.

Euston Station c1837

While Michael was still working at Euston, Eliza, now pregnant with their fifth child, was also coping with one of the twins – young James – who was a sickly child. James died in January 1839 – a tragedy which greatly hastened Michael's determination to apply for a job at Tring, where his family could enjoy a healthier life.

Soon after James's death, Michael landed his coveted job at Tring and the family moved into one of the newly-built railway workers' cottages in this small, prosperous Hertfordshire market town situated on the old Roman Akeman Street, linking London to Cirencester. Michael remained a porter until 1847 when he was promoted as a ticket inspector, earning a starting wage of £1/10/-, rising to £1/30/-, with his own office – quite a promotion from being a lowly porter.

Thomasine, meanwhile, continued to live with her grand-

The Tring railway workers' cottages

parents at Stoke Prior, but Michael and Eliza hoped she could return to them soon.

****

In1840 a very Stoke Prior family conclave was held at the home of Eliza's parents, James and Ann Preece. Present were Michael and Eliza, Eliza's elder sister, Mary Price (the younger generation seem to have preferred to spell their surname "Price"), and an old family friend, Sir William Keith Ball – "Uncle Keith" (see Chapter 1). The business of the conclave was to plan the future upbringing of the two eldest Meredith children: Thomasine and Henry. It was decided that they, at least, no matter how many more Meredith children were born, should be given the upbringing and education that they would have received had Michael's father not dribbled his handsome estate away in drink and gambling.[10] So young Henry, then aged six, was to be sent immediately to live in London with his aunt Mary Price. (Henry was later sent to a public school and then studied medicine at the Royal College of Surgeons.)

Thomasine, aged seven, was to go back to live with her parents at Tring for two years, after which she was to join Henry in London, living in the rather grand double-fronted, four-storey house at 40 Fitzroy Street, Marylebone, which her aunt Mary Price shared with Sir William Keith Ball when he was in town.

After leaving Stoke Prior and then living in Tring for the next two years, Thomasine, being a willing little girl, and happy to be with her mother and father, knuckled down to helping her mother with the housework in their railway company cottage. She got to know some of the children from the other families in the row of cottages, and also greatly enjoyed her father's riding lessons when he hired a pony for her from a local farm – as he had years before with young Eliza. She also enjoyed listening to the organ during the Sunday morning church services at St Peter and St Paul's where she discovered her early love of music. During that time her mother gave birth in 1841 to another daughter, named Eliza.

Big excitement occurred in November 1844 when 25-year-old Queen Victoria, with Prince Albert and their retinue, stopped at Tring station on their first train trip north. *The Illustrated London News* of November 16th 1844, reported the event:

The Royal Train in 1844

"The drizzling rain which was falling at the time had not deterred a considerable number of persons from collecting together at Tring station. The station is situated 31¾ miles from London, and was reached at 14 minutes past ten o'clock; and here the train halted for a few minutes, in order that the engine might obtain a fresh supply of water.

Among the persons assembled at this station were the juvenile members of the neighbouring population, boys and girls, who were drawn up in distinct rows, and who strained their tiny voices to be utmost in welcoming their Sovereign. Her Majesty appeared highly pleased with this specimen of infantine loyalty and enthusiasm. A sufficient supply of water having been obtained, the train again started on its course, at 18 minutes past ten o'clock..."[11]

William Meredith, aged eight, was one of the "tiny voices" who serenaded the Queen that day, but Thomasine, now 11, missed the Queen's visit to Tring because, at the age of nine, as planned by the family conclave, she had joined her brother, Henry, in London to live in the rather grand house at 40 Fitzroy Street where she was "adopted" by her aunt, Mary Price, who was listed as "spinster" and "householder" in the Census, and who was in charge of the household and a number of servants, while

Sir William Keith came and went on business and church interests.

Thomasine was provided with a governess who gave her a good education[12] before she was sent as a teenager to a Paris finishing school for two years to prepare her for marriage to a suitable young man

Most of Thomasine's time at finishing school was spent learning the finer points of being a lady: how to dress for a ball, a wedding, an afternoon tea, how to instruct servants in the correct way to set a table for a banquet, and how a lady should enter a room gracefully – and to depart equally gracefully. Madame, the headmistress, or 'principale', was very strict, but she taught her students to speak good French – and Thomasine particularly enjoyed the music lessons. She and her fellow students were even taken to the Paris Opera a couple of times.

Returning to London, Thomasine was taken to lunches and afternoon tea parties by her Aunt and carefully introduced to suitable young men. Because she had no inheritance, a suitable match was likely to be a young curate, and indeed Thomasine in 1851 married a curate, the Rev. Edward James Cooper, at St Mary's church, Marylebone, and went to live with him in Garforth, Yorkshire, where he later became vicar.

At first, it was a lonely existence for Thomasine with no family living nearby, and she suspected that in her absence certain family members had not been supportive. In a letter[13] to her younger brother, William (who, having joined the railways at the age of 13, was now away at sea with the Navy), written from her home in Yorkshire in 1860, Thomasine wrote:

> I cannot help thinking either that Mother does not care for me, or that someone has set her against me or they would write oftener. Harry seemed quite to have taken a hatred to me... when I was in town last, I know that is Louisa's fault, but why

mother should be so cool, I can't think for I am sure I never did anything to deserve it. ...I cannot ask Mother straight forward whether she is offended with me, and what for, because I can never be sure that only Father and her will see my letter so I want you dear William first to write, but if you see Father by himself sometime ask him if there is any reason for Mother's not writing to me... Forgive this stupid scrawl all about disagreeable things but you are the only one I can open my mind to. ... what a pity Harry and Louisa threw away their chance through idleness and extravagance! Because I tried to advise Harry to use his talents and profession, that is what he dislikes me for and through Louisa speaking against me and Eliza, she had made him say to my very face that he hated us both. However I feel quite certain that I never deserved either Harry's dislike or Mother's coolness, I must rest content till time shall work a change in their opinions."

This ill-feeling between mother and daughter was to abate as time went on, but at that stage of her life, Thomasine felt very lonely and vulnerable.

But gradually Thomasine's self-reliant and resilient nature helped her to make friends among the parishioners. Coping with a damp, draughty manse was difficult with virtually no domestic help, and Thomasine also soon found she was pregnant. She and Edward James had five children over the next few years, one of whom, Amelia, died in 1861 at three years and eight months from Scarlet Fever.

In another letter to her brother William (undated, but from its contents *circa* early 1862), Thomasine discusses the vague possibility that the family might manage, with the help of a lawyer, to recover some of the funds from the former estate of her grandfather, Michael Meredith Snr. which had been held in Chancery since 1850. (Nothing further came of this matter until many years later.)

Her husband, Edward, died a year later, from a lingering illness following Scarlet Fever. He and Thomasine had come to London and were temporarily staying in lodgings, perhaps close to where he was receiving medical treatment. Edward's death left Thomasine, at the age of 29, a widow with her four surviving young children. She returned home to Yorkshire, not knowing what she and her children would do next.

It was then that Sir William Keith Ball and Mary Price came to her rescue, and Thomasine and her four children were invited to come back to London from Yorkshire to live in a house Sir Keith owned, not far from his new residence in Bayswater.

END NOTES CHAPTER 2

[1] In the Will lodged in Hereford Records and Archive Centre, Hereford, UK, dated 1774, Richard Evans decreed that after disposing of certain Stoke Prior property to his sister, Rebecca Maund, the bulk of his estates in several parishes and townships such as Stoke Prior, Humber and Risbury were to be bequeathed to his illegitimate son, Michael (Meredith) when he reached the age of 21. Until he reached the age of 15 Michael was to receive £25 year to

pay for his education and maintenance, and from the age of 15 to 21 he was to receive the proceeds of the rentals from the late Richard's properties.

[2] The Will went on: *"...until he shall attain his Age of twenty one years And from and after such his Attainment and subject to the said Term I give devise and bequeath unto the said Michael Meredith All my Freehold and Leasehold Estates."*

Michael's mother, Ann Meredith, was not forgotten. The Will stipulated:

"I give and bequeath unto my servant Ann Meredith if she shall be living at the time of my Decease All my Household Goods Clothes Plates Linen Wearing Apparel and all my Stock of Cattle Grain and other Effects which shall be in or upon my Dwelling house and Lands and other Houses and Lands in my possession in the parish of Stoke Prior."

The Executors of the Will were George Terry, John Powles and Henry Maund. After Richard Edward's death in 1778 when Michael was only four, Ann Meredith married Henry Maund's son, William, in April 1778 and had five further children by him – yet another example of how Stoke Prior families stuck together and kept their money safe.

[3] Molina's grandfather was William Greenwood (1712-92), who married Mary Carpenter (1713-74). They had 11 children, one of whom was Thomas Greenwood (1745-1814), who married Mary Yates (1743-1830), and had two daughters, Molina (1773-1819) and Lucy (1777-1846). (Ref: *Ancestry*.)

[4] Richard was born in 1799 and nothing more of him is known.

[5] There was a third son, Henry, two years younger than Michael. He apparently was not strong and died young, date unknown.

[6] Michael senior died in 1833 and had been living in a residence called *Humber* in Stoke Prior with his half-brother, Wiliam Maund. His entire estate finally went into Chancery in 1855.

[7] *Housing Rents, Housing Quality, and Living Standards in England and Wales, 1640-1909* Gregory Clark University of California, Davis (gclark@ucdavis.edu) October, 1999

[8] Railway Mania was a frenzy of speculation which reached its peak in the 1840s. The new, so fast, railway means of transportation made the old canals look redundant, and with the pace of business quickening as the Victorian era began, the price of railway shares sky-rocketed until the inevitable collapse. It reached its peak in 1846, when 272 Acts of Parliament were passed, setting up new railway companies, with a total of 9,500 miles (15,300km) of new railways proposed, but about one third of these never materialised. Many of

the investment companies either collapsed or were bought out by larger competitors. Finally only very large railway companies existed, and Railway Mania went the same way as Tulip Mania had gone.

[9] Euston Station was a grand establishment with its Doric-columned portico entrance. Technically it was state-of-the art with its platforms, engine houses, passenger sheds, booking offices, coke vaults, and even the track leading out of the station lit by gas, provided by the adjacent gasworks.

[10] William, the third surviving child, was not to get such favoured treatment. He started work on the railways at Paddington, aged 13, before joining the Royal Navy in 1855, aged 17, serving first on the *Illustrious* and later joining the *Pearl* in Hong Kong. By 1891 he had emigrated to Canada, married a Canadian girl, Susannah Cruse, and died in Halifax, Canada in 1907

[11] The Royal train took a speedy 52 minutes to journey from London to Tring, and after that stop the Queen ordered the train driver to slow down. The Queen's visit to Tring might have alerted the satirical poet Edward Lear who wrote a limerick about the town in his *Book of Nonsense* (1846
There was an Old Person of Tring,
Who embellished his nose with a ring;
He gazed at the moon every evening in June,
That ecstatic Old Person of Tring.

[12] *Two Families.op cit.*

3

"Uncle Keith"

SIR WILLIAM KEITH BALL has always been counted as "family" by the Stoke Prior clans – indeed, some of his own family came from the area. "Uncle Keith", as they all called him, was something of an enigma, being on the one hand a fairy godfather to many of the Stoke Prior people, yet at the same time an astute businessman and consummate wheeler-dealer. He was the second baronet, the only son and only child of a highly-distinguished naval officer, Sir Alexander Ball, who was a close friend of Admiral Nelson. When he and Nelson had first met, Nelson had taken a dislike to Ball, regarding him as a dandy, but subsequently, in late May 1798, after setting off from Gibraltar in a fierce storm with Nelson commanding the *Vanguard* and Ball commanding the *Alexander,* the *Vanguard* lost its fore and top masts. The two ships were tied together, to tow the damaged ship, and at one point Nelson ordered the *Alexander* to let go the tow rope, but Ball disobeyed the order and towed the *Vanguard* to safe harbour in Sardinia. Thereafter they were firm friends and the existing letters from Nelson to Ball are full of affection. Alexander Ball was appointed Civil Administrator of Malta from 1799 to 1800 and again in 1802 until his death on October 25th 1809. His support of the Maltese, who were fighting the French, won him the affection of the Maltese who clapped and cheered him whenever he went about his business on the island.[1]

His son, William Keith Ball, had inherited the title and the same lovable characteristics which had made his father so favoured by the Maltese. Keith, as everyone called him, was born in 1788, attended Christ Church Oxford for a month or two before matriculating in 1807 and then going on the obligatory Grand Tour of Europe before inheriting the baronetcy when he was 20 on the death in Malta of his father in 1809. After his father's death, young Keith wrote from Malta to King George III, extolling his late father's service to King and Country and requesting the King grant him remuneration suitable for the maintenance of his rank in society. His Majesty complied with this request, granting him the very handsome sum of £600 a year until 1856. Sir William Keith then returned to London to live with his widowed mother at 41 Queen Anne Street, Westminster, until her death in 1831 when, probably inheriting some money from her, he bought the lease on yet another prestige address: 42 Upper Seymour Street, Portman Square, where he lived, on-and-off, for many years. By this time Keith was investing in property not only in London but also Cape Breton with some of his cousins, and in Calcutta and Nova Scotia[2]. He also inherited a pub from a woman who had been a witness at his parents' wedding. All the while, he was also a very religious man, having studied Divinity at Oxford and becoming a lay clergyman later in life. His friendship with the Prices (Preeces) from Stoke Prior went back a long way; he was mentioned in the Census of 1841 as being present with members of the Price family, and again, in the Census of 1851, he was listed along with the Prices, including Thomasine (then aged 18), at a gathering for a family wedding.

****

Meanwhile, back at Tring, Michael and Eliza were content, and more Meredith babies continued to arrive: Louisa, was born in 1843, but died after a few days (they later named another daughter Louisa); Mary was born in 1844; Edward in 1847; Frederick in1849; Rowland Joseph in 1851 and another Louisa in 1856. Despite their relative happiness at Tring, something still unsettled Michael, particularly when he was helping with the horses in the big Hertfordshire country estates. His family estate had been larger…what a pity his father had been so degenerate.

By the time he reached 55 in 1858, still with seven children aged between 15 and infancy on his hands, Michael started to panic. The New Poor Law, passed in 1834, only provided for destitute people relegated to the workhouse and there was yet to be a retirement pension for most workers, including those employed by the railways.

What seemed at the time to be a godsend arrived in a letter from their son Henry who had recently emigrated to New

Zealand and was now working as a surgeon with the (British) 65th Regiment of the Auckland Battalion on New Zealand's North Island.

Henry had emigrated with his young wife, Louisa Rosamond de Montmorency, who had just given birth to their second son, William, following the death in London of their first son, Hildebrand Keith. Henry had taken this big step because he had realised that despite his abilities as a surgeon, he had little chance of advancing far in the English medical profession where money and birth paved the way to success. (In Thomasine's opinion, Henry was lazy and profligate). As the son of a railway worker (even with the support of Sir William Keith Ball), and with no vast fortune behind him, it was better to travel to a new land and establish himself there. He was now on the point of leaving the Army to set up private practice in Wellington.

He urged his parents to migrate to Auckland where they could obtain a government grant of good agricultural land and set up a farm and prosper. New Zealand, he told his parents, was a strikingly beautiful land with snow-capped mountains, great forests, and grassy plains where sheep graze. Wool was becoming a big money-spinner.

There was only a handful of British settled there yet, but Henry, a relative newcomer, could discern little trouble with the native Maoris – Polynesians who came down from the Pacific islands in canoes maybe 1000 years ago. At that time there were only about 130,000 British settlers there but they had the support of the British Army to protect them if any troubles were to break out.

END NOTES CHAPTER 3

[1] *Dictionary of National Biography.*

[2] His father, Sir Alexander, had served for three years in the British Navy's Newfoundland Division during his earlier naval career and may well have purchased land or other interests there.

4

New Zealand

ON AUGUST 20th 1859, the Meredith family arrived at Gravesend, carrying their only worldly goods, and strode expectantly up the gangplank of the 846-ton passenger part steam, part-sailing ship, *Nourmahal*, and climbed down to steerage class, to set sail for New Zealand. They were not prepared for what they were to experience: sailing steerage along with 120 or so of the ship's 150-odd passengers

The voyage to New Zealand from England was the longest migration route in the world. The *Nourmahal* rolled and plunged through fearsome waves in the Bay of Biscay and across the Atlantic towards South America, then swung back wide round the Cape of Good Hope into the Roaring Forties – westerly winds that blew ships along at great speed. It was to take the Meredith family 108 days (just over three-and-a-half months). Their daily allocated rations of food – salted and preserved meat, ship's biscuits, flour, oatmeal, and dried potatoes – was inedible, and conditions below deck were foul. The ship ploughed through storms, and the waves broke over the decks and washed down into steerage class on many occasions. It was a tough voyage.

However, the tedium of the voyage was alleviated by the shipboard romance of their daughter, Eliza, and a young fellow passenger, Edward Richards. The love-stricken young couple decided they would start their new life together in New Zealand, and a fellow passenger, the Rev Samuel Blackburn (who was travelling to New Zealand to take up the position of Principal of St. Johns College, Auckland) married the young passengers, providing a welcome diversion for all on board.[1]

Arriving in New Zealand, and with the help of Henry, Michael applied for a government grant of a Section of 10 acres of good farming land at Ramarama (also called Shepherd's Bush), not far from the town of Drury, south of Auckland. With the help of some of the local settlers, who always rallied around newcomers, Michael and his now 12 year old son, Frederick, cut down trees and cleared their land for sheep and cattle grazing and crops of corn. Again with the help of their neighbours, they built a sturdy wooden house with three bedrooms and a main room with a kitchen. They had left behind the Industrial Revolution for a more gentle, agrarian life – or so they hoped.

Despite Henry's glowing accounts of life in New Zealand, trouble was brewing. The 1840s had seen many inter-tribal battles, sometimes called the "Musket Wars". Sporadic conflicts between the British and the Maori also broke out. The Maoris, although already heavily outnumbered by the British Army, had quickly developed a sophisticated form of guerrilla warfare based on their ancient knowledge of the forests and foliage of New Zealand. To further enhance their military tactics, the Maoris had not only adopted the English musket but had then outstripped the British by purchasing from an Australian trader double-barrelled cap guns, which the British Army was not equipped with until later. [2]

Since 1856 race relations had become a major problem. Responsible government had been introduced by then, but Governor Gore Browne decided to keep native affairs under his personal control. Race relations were exacerbated by the increasing pressure by the colonists who wanted more of the Maori land.

During the Merediths' first year in New Zealand the First Taranaki War (March 17th 1860 to March 18th 1861) broke out in the Taranaki area to the south-west of Auckland over land ownership and the imposition of British sovereignty on the Maori population. The war was to continue for a year there, involving more than 3,500 imperial troops brought in from Australia, plus volunteers from the local community, versus around 1500 Maori men, women and children. The war ended in a ceasefire, with neither side admitting defeat.

An uneasy truce was negotiated, but Governor Thomas Gore Browne, was determined to completely defeat the Maori King movement (see Appendix A). For the next 18 months it looked as if further war had been averted.

But then, in March 1863, two years after Michael and Eliza and family arrived in New Zealand, Governor Grey, who had taken over from Browne, went to Taranaki and re-occupied the

Maori territory there. A series of relatively minor battles ensued, and a number of Maoris and British troops were killed. After that, Taranaki was deemed to have quietened down and most of the British troops were moved to Auckland and the Waikato area to its south. Next,[3] on July 9th 1863, Grey issued a proclamation addressed to seven Maori tribes: "All persons of the native race living in this Manukau district, and the Waikato frontier, are hereby requested immediately to take the Oath of Allegiance to Her Majesty the Queen and to give up their arms to an officer appointed by Government for that purpose. Natives who comply with this order will be protected."

On the same day, in reference to the news that the Maori Kingites were planning a bloodthirsty attack on Auckland, Grey also proclaimed that because it was impossible for the police and military at night time to distinguish between "friends and foes" "It is therefore required of all friendly disposed Maoris, that they abide within their houses from dusk in the evening until daybreak; order them not move about outside, lest they get into trouble.

"It has also been ordered that every Maori found on the streets of the town after dark, be apprehended." Two days later, on July 11th, Grey ordered the invasion of the Kingite territories[4] Up till then, in the more central area just south of Auckland where the Merediths were living, despite some signs of discontent among the Maoris, the Merediths and their neighbours in Ramarama and Drury had been quietly getting on with their farming business, comfortable in the knowledge that the Auckland 65th Regiment was nearby and regularly making patrols around the area. Most of the settlers didn't yet even own guns themselves, content in the belief the Army would look after them in an emergency. However, events were moving inexorably towards war in their part of the North Island.

****

After three and a half years in Ramarama, Michael's crops were yielding corn and their cows producing good milk. The two older girls, Eliza and Mary, were getting on with their married lives, and baby Louisa was now seven and a pupil at the local school in Drury. The Merediths and their neighbours were contentedly getting on with their lives, but serious trouble was brewing. (See Appendix A for more details.)

****

On July 14th, three days after Governor Grey ordered the invasion of the Maori Kingite-held territories in the Waikato, Michael and Frederick, now 14, were busy fencing-in and clearing the farthest section of their land in a bushy area next to the Great South Road. That morning Eliza farewelled them from the front door of their little house and proudly watched them walk down the road in their brand-new moleskin trousers. That was the last time she saw either of them alive.

As they shaped the fence pegs, Michael and Frederick were completely unaware that four young Maori braves from an up-river tribe were hiding in the undergrowth by the road, waiting for the sound of a patrol of the 65th Regiment which was scheduled to march down from Auckland that morning. On hearing the marching boots of the regiment, they were to signal to the rest of their tribe to launch an attack,

Then they caught sight of Michael and Frederick, working close to the road. The young Maoris swiftly realised that their fellow tribesmen's plan to ambush the Army patrol would be foiled were these settlers to issue a warning of their presence to the soldiers. In a flash, three of the Maoris leaped from the bushes, and with blood-curdling yells, grabbed Michael and Frederick by their necks. Michael turned and managed to knock his assailant to the ground, whereupon the fourth young Maori leaped from the bushes and in turn tackled Michael to the ground. The four braves then dragged the hapless man and his son into a copse of trees, picking up the axe and tomahawk on the way.

The struggle ended when both Michael and Frederick lay unconscious on the ground while the Maoris hacked at their skulls with the tomahawk and axe. Michael's brain was exposed to the morning sunlight while Frederick's face and head were viciously hacked too. Blood gushed from both victims while the young Maoris tore off Michael's brand- new moleskin trousers, leaving him almost naked, lying on the ground. Next, they stripped off Frederick's moleskin trousers too but left both men's shoes behind – too old to be coveted. They then dragged both bodies through the undergrowth to a tree out of sight of the road and the soon-to-be-passing soldiers. They then flitted back into the undergrowth and re-joined their fellow tribesmen, who, having seen what had happened, abandoned any further attempt to attack the army patrol that day.

On learning the dreadful news, Eliza was, of course, distraught. The neighbours took her and the two children into their home for the night. The Army sent out patrols and recovered the bodies.

Before the funeral took place, the Coroner's Inquest[5] was held on July 17th in a store hut at the 65th Regiment's Drury camp before Major Speedy, RM, coroner for the district. The list of injuries sustained by Michael and Frederick makes harrowing reading.

James Crimmins, drummer of the 65th Regiment, told the Inquest how he accompanied the search party the morning after the Regiment had been alerted of Michael and Frederick's absence the previous evening. He told how he blew his bugle, still believing Michael and Frederick were alive. Then a civilian led him to the bodies. He continued sounding his bugle because he assumed the attack had been by "natives" and he believed that by sounding his bugle, any natives still in the vicinity would assume there was a large body of soldiers, which would deter them from attacking them.

Sergeant Brown began his report by describing arriving early the next morning at the clearing where Michael and Frederick had been cutting timber rails for their fence: "We discovered some iron wedges for splitting wood, and on searching round the place we discovered the bodies of the man and boy lying at the trunk of a tree, convenient to where they were working...They had wounds from an axe or a tomahawk. The man's face was knocked in. The bodies were mutilated as they now appear. The wounds were sufficient to cause death."

Joseph Meredith, Michael's 12-year-old son, who was among the search party of civilians who first discovered the bodies, was then called to give his account of the matter. He described what he saw: "We did not find my father's trousers; the boots were lying at his feet. The trousers were a new pair of moleskins; the boots were old. My brother wore a tweed jacket, the same as I wear, and moleskin trousers…"

At the end of the Inquest the jury returned a verdict of "wilful murder". The perpetrators of these acts were deemed to be by "person or persons unknown". The Army sent out a large, mounted, search party to look for the murderers and 18 Maoris were arrested, amongst them the Chief, Ihaka.

What was the reason for this brutal attack, the Inquest deliberated? Could the altercation – over a wandering pig – between Michael and the frail old tribal leader, Simons, of Tuimata, have triggered such a vicious onslaught? This was the theory held by some of the settlers. At the Inquest, the local bootmaker, described how Frederick had come a month earlier, on June 10th, to his house for two pairs of boots to be repaired. One pair of them was now on the body of one of the victims, the bootmaker said. He went on to relate that while Frederick waited for the boots, he told him about his father's quarrel with the chief. He and his father, a day or two before, had gone and fetched the pig away from the native ground at the Maori settlement. They fetched the pig home. Simons, the chief, came back to his father's house, when he found the pig was taken away, and demanded it, and £5 damages for the pig eating their potatoes and kumeras. His father refusing, Simons sent his young men and took the pig away during his father's absence.

Whether this quarrel over a pig had been a factor in causing the attack, or whether the sight of Michael and Frederick busily fencing in their section had touched a sensitive nerve in the Maoris who were already reacting across the North Island to the imposition of British sovereignty and the growing land claims of the settlers, was never determined.

Ultimately, it was confirmed that the four young Maoris who carried out the attack were the *avant garde* of a posse of Maoris planning to attack the patrol of the 65th Regiment due to pass along the road that morning. Michael and Frederick had simply got in their way.[6]

The *Southern Cross* newspaper of July 15th 1863, reporting the Inquest, concluded[7] "The victims were harmless settlers, but it shows that the natives mean to make this a war of races."

The *Hawkes Bay Herald* on July 27th 1863, reporting the advance into Waikato, said: "We perceive, although not mentioned in the letter of our correspondent, the advance into the Waikato was consequent upon a brutal murder committed upon a settler named Meredith and his son."

The Meredith murders, although not the cause, were yet another symptom or factor in events leading to the ensuing deadly war in the Waikato which was a major event in the New Zealand Wars. which were to continue until 1872. The ensuing Waikato conflict, lasting 15 months, was, as historian James Belich put it: "the largest and most important of the New Zealand Wars".[8]

After the funeral, Eliza returned to her house to find it totally ransacked and the livestock either slaughtered or stolen. Shattered by the whole ghastly event, she decided to leave the farm forever – joining many other settlers who were warned to come into the safety of the town.

Eliza Meredith after the murder.
Her formerly sweet mouth has
taken on a harder line.

The murder of Michael and Frederick Meredith was not, as some have claimed, the cause of the New Zealand Wars, but it contributed to the general unease of the British settlers and strengthened their resolve to fight and overwhelm the Maoris in the nine years of battle to come.

If he had known what was in store for him, would the 16-year-old Michael Meredith have turned back home to *The Heath* on that spring day in 1819 when he had been setting off to seek his fortune in London?

END NOTES CHAPTER 4

[1] The shipping list published in the *New Zealander* on December 7th 1859 lists "Arrived Auckland Michael, Eliza Meredith with children Eliza, Mary, Ed. Charles, Frederick Richard, Rowland Joseph and Rosamond."

[2] Cowan, James, T*he New Zealand Wars: Ch. 7.[Cowan.]*

[3] *Cowan ibid.*

[4] *Cowan ibid.*

[5] A full report of the Inquest was published in the *Daily Southern Cross*, July 18th 1863. p4. "The Shepherd's Bush Murder" (*sic*). Inquest on the Bodies. (From our Special Correspondent.). Camp. Drury, July 17th, 1863.

[6]. *Daily Southern Cross, ibid.*

[6] On November 25th 1863 the *New Zealand Herald* published a list of the Maori chiefs killed or captured at Rangiriri. The report said: "Tarahawaiki, the murderer of Mr. Meredith was taken."

[8] Ref *The Victorian Interpretation of Racial Conflict* by James Belich, McGill-Queen's University Press, p119. Approximately 27 settlers were killed in the conflict. [*Victorian Interpretation.*]

5

London

BACK IN LONDON it is now late October 1863, just a month since Walter "Jack" Browne has broken the tragic news to Thomasine of the murder of her father Michael, and brother Frederick, in New Zealand.

Sitting on the open top of one of those new-fangled omnibuses which have been introduced in London during his absence in India, Jack is ruminating over his future.

I can't go on accepting Uncle Keith's hospitality for much longer, he thinks, as the omnibus clip-clops past the few remaining old houses and the new shops in Oxford Street. *I must decide whether to go back to India – my sisters would welcome me there now they're married and living in Calcutta.*

But, no. I'm done with India. I need a new challenge.

The omnibus slows down and the driver pulls up his horses at a stop while several passengers get on and find seats in the warmer, enclosed lower deck. But one new passenger begins to climb up the steps at the back of the vehicle, while the driver waits patiently.

As the passenger climbs up to the top deck, Jack observes a feather first, then a black straw hat with a black veil. *She must be an intrepid lady to brave the steps and the cold air on the top of an omnibus,* Jack thinks as he stands up to offer her assistance. He looks down at the woman, who is clad all in black, clinging on to the handrail while juggling several large parcels.

"May I assist you, Madam?" he asks. The woman looks up, and through her veil, Jack sees that it is Thomasine.

"Tommy!" he exclaims. "Here, pass up those boxes to me and I'll help you get seated before the omnibus moves off".

Stepping agilely up the last few steps, Thomasine lifts the veil off her face and smiles. "Thank you, Jack! Fancy meeting you again – on an omnibus!"[1]

"Come and sit next to me, Tommy, and tell me what you've been doing. I've been wanting to get in touch with you again, but I didn't like to intrude at such a sad time."

Thomasine settles herself on one of the seats that run back to back along the middle of the top of the omnibus. Stowing her parcels under the seat, she turns to Jack: "I've been shopping here in Regent and Oxford Streets for winter clothes for the children – they grow so fast!"

As the omnibus rolls on up Oxford Street, Jack feels a glow of pleasure at encountering "Tommy" again. She hasn't really changed so very much since he first knew her – although there is a sadness in her eyes that is new to him.

"Having to do the shopping for new clothes for the children has helped to take my mind off the dreadful event of my father and brother's deaths – murders, I should say. I found some clothes for the older children at Dickens & Smith[2] in Regent Street and then I wandered around the little drapery shops in Oxford Street, trying to find some bargains, specially something suitable for myself to wear. I hear that a new department store called John Lewis is to open in Oxford Street next year, so that will be a help," she says. "But I must say I'm so tired of wearing these old black clothes. I was just coming to the end of the mourning period for my dear husband, Edward, and now I'm in mourning for my father and brother."

"It's refreshing to see a woman braving the steps of an omnibus – and the cold wind – to come up and sit on top of one," Jack observes.

"I can't stand the stuffiness of the lower decks of omnibuses," Thomasine replies, looking out at the passing shops as the horses clopped along. "I would wager those new underground trains must be extremely stuffy! Have you travelled in one yet?"

"Yes," replies Jack, beaming at the memory. "I have indeed! And they're quite marvellous. I happened to travel on the Underground on the very first day the Metropolitan Line opened last January[3]. The first underground railway in the world! I needed to visit my solicitor in the City, so Farringdon, the last station on the new Underground line, was an ideal station to alight. There was an enormous crowd that first day – so many people wanting to experience the phenomenon of travelling so deep underground. The only drawback I could notice was the sooty smoke from the engine that wafted into the carriage at certain stations. But they say that can be rectified. I've since taken the underground railway several times to travel to the City. I must say I do enjoy new experiences."

Thomasine is amused at Jack's enthusiasm. *He hasn't changed a bit,* she thinks, *although he's now a grown man – and a handsome one at that!*

"We're both heading home in the same direction, I was planning to get off the omnibus in Bayswater Road and walk to Uncle Keith's in Leinster Gardens," Jack says. "Could I take you for a cup of tea in the little teashop around the corner from your place? I know you are now engaged to marry Uncle Keith, but he wouldn't mind my inviting you to a teashop, would he?"

"Of course not!" Thomasine laughs. "Keith wouldn't mind in the slightest. He's such a sweetie. He's only offered to marry me because he's a gallant gentleman and he regards me, a widow with four young children to support, as a damsel in distress. After all, he's 75!"

The omnibus finally arrives at their destination, and Jack helps Thomasine with her parcels and boxes down the steps and onto the pavement. The little teashop is just around the corner, a haven from the biting wind that is blowing dead Autumn leaves along the street. A few specks and spatters of rain are starting to fall, and the bright oil lamp lights of the teashop send out a welcome glow.

As they wait for the waitress to bring their tea and scones, Jack asks Thomasine how her mother, Eliza, is coping with the shock of Michael's and Frederick's murders.

"I've had a letter from my sister, Mary, who says Mother has come to live with her now. The farmhouse has been totally wrecked by vandals, and the livestock stolen. Mother is apparently completely shattered by what has happened, and Mary doesn't think she'll ever go back to the farm. I gather most of the other farmers in the district have moved into the safety of Auckland now that war is raging in their area.

"My mother is a very strong woman and she will manage. But Michael was her life. She'll never be the same without him."

The waitress brings their scones and pot of tea and Jack offers to pour it.

"It's all dreadfully, dreadfully awful," Thomasine adds. "But let's not talk about it anymore. Tell me about what you've been up to all these years."

"Well," Jack begins. "As I mentioned that day – when I brought you the news about your father and brother – after finishing my schooling at 16, I went out to India, desperate to fight in the Indian Mutiny – I've always been fascinated with the army. Two of my sisters, Mary Anne and Harriet Agnes, later married employees of the old East India Company, and they have been keen for me to come out again and join them.

"By the time I got there, the Indian Mutiny was more-or-less over and the country was about to be administered directly by the British Government – the British Raj. I joined the British Army, serving in the ranks – not as an officer like my brother William later did – he's a lieutenant-colonel. I was useful to the Army because I was a good horseman, a so-called 'rough rider', and I had learned sufficient medical skills from my father – he had trained as a doctor as a young man – so I could also work as a medical orderly when trouble occurred. I became proficient in stemming wounds and setting broken bones. But most of the major fighting was over and I couldn't see any long-term future there, and my father agreed to pay me out, So here I am, back in England and wondering what to do with the rest of my life."

Thomasine looks at him sympathetically. He was always so bright and full of purpose when she'd known him at Stoke Prior, but now he seems uncharacteristically unsure of himself.

The teashop clock chimes four and Thomasine sits up, startled. "I must dash!" she exclaims. "The children's nanny will be waiting for me. It's almost time for their tea! Jack, it's been really good to see you again. Could we meet again another day for a cup of tea?"

Jack smiles. "Of course, Tommy," he says. "How would next Tuesday at 3 pm, here, suit you?"

Thomasine agrees to meet him. "I look forward to hearing more about your adventures in India," she adds.

"And I want to hear about your life as a parson's wife in Yorkshire," he says.

"Not as exciting a story as yours," Thomasine laughs as she gathers up her parcels and sets off back home, and Jack returns to Uncle Keith's grand five-storeys-plus-basement residence in Leinster Gardens.

Sir William Keith Ball's house at 33 Leinster Gardens, Bayswater (the house with the white door – centre)

The following Tuesday it is raining again, but harder, and Thomasine scurries along the street, her umbrella bobbing back and forth in the wind. Once again, the lamplight of the teashop beckons, and she pushes the door. Its bell tinkles and she steps in. Jack is already there, seated at a window table, not far from the fire blazing in the fireplace.

"Come and sit beside me, Tommy, it's nice and warm here," Jack says, getting up to take her coat and gesturing to the waitress to bring tea and scones. The waitress puts a pot of tea and a plate of scones on the table in front of them and Jack and Thomasine both start to speak at once.

"Sorry, Tommy," Jack apologises, "But there's just so much to talk about! You promised to tell me about your life in Yorkshire…"

"Well," Thomasine begins, "As I said, it's not nearly as exciting as your experiences in India must have been. As you know, my parents – Michael and Eliza – had many children – 15 in all, although only nine survived. and I had been sent to live with my grandparents at Stoke Prior until I was seven, then I returned to my family at Tring for two years, before being 'adopted' by Mary Price and going to live with her and Uncle Keith in London. After I came back from finishing school in

Paris I went on living in London with Uncle Keith and dear Aunt Mary Price, God bless her soul – she passed away in October 1856. She was like a mother to me and she had me educated by a very qualified governess. I was being prepared for a good marriage, but as I didn't have a fortune behind me, as some of the girls at the finishing school did, a member of the clergy was regarded as an ideal match. Uncle Keith knew so many church members."

"Tell me about the Paris finishing school," Jack interrupts. "What was it like?"

"Well," Thomasine begins, "we learned all the social graces. The number of times I had to enter a room elegantly, pausing after the door was opened, then gracefully gliding in! But what I enjoyed most was on certain afternoons when Madame was taking her siesta, one of the younger teachers, a Parisienne named Claire, would help me and my friend, Maisie, to sneak out of the schoolhouse and she would take us down to Montmartre to visit some artists she knew there. It was a revelation to me to enter their studios, to smell the oil paint and to see the naked models posing for the artists, and then Claire would take us to a coffee shop and we would sit at a table out on the footpath and watch the passing parade on the boulevard. I thoroughly enjoyed my time in Paris!"

"And then what happened?" asks Jack.

"I returned to London, and when I was 19, I was introduced to Edward James Cooper, a young curate from Devises in Yorkshire. We married a year-or-so later, in1853. I found him a gentle, companionable man with a lot of inner strength. Dear Edward, bless him. As time went on and the babies arrived, we were able to move into the vicarage after Edward became the Vicar, and at least we had some more space to live in.

"But the vicarage was damp and very cold, and the children were constantly ill. I only had a maid, so there was a lot to do to keep the household in shape with four young children to look after, and with them being so often ill."

Jack leans towards her and squeezes her hand. "My poor Tommy, it sounds thoroughly miserable!"

"There was a bright side to it all," Thomasine continues. "I learned how to play the church organ – I already could play the piano quite well – and I played the hymns at Sunday services, which I thoroughly enjoyed. And I used to travel around the town in a pony trap, visiting parishioners. I got to know virtually everybody in the town, learning about their lives and their problems. It took me back to my days as a child at Stoke Prior.

"Then my second eldest, Amelia, fell dreadfully ill with the Scarlet Fever. It was already starting to be an epidemic two years ago. Did you know that at least 30,000 people have died from it since then? Amelia died. It came as a devastating shock to me. How could the Lord have allowed that beautiful young child to pass away?" Thomasine's voice trembles. "We were just about to move at last to the new vicarage, which would have been dry and warm, when my dear husband, James, too, caught the Fever and died. I was carrying my fifth child, Herbert James, who was born after his father died. So there I was, with a new baby and my three other surviving children, with nowhere to go. My whole existence fell apart and only my faith in God kept me going. And then Keith came to my rescue and provided a comfortable house with servants here in London for me and the children – the house you visited when you brought the news of my father and brother.

"So that's my story, it's not very exciting" she concludes.

Jack clasps her hand again for a moment. "Poor, poor, Tommy," he says. "You didn't deserve such a life. You were always the brightest, liveliest person at the Stoke Prior gatherings, so full of laughter and witty chatter."

Thomasine smiles gently. "Well," she says, "at least I had a good marriage, which is more than a lot of women can say. And now it's your turn, Jack. Tell me, first of all, how you came to be a close friend of Sir William Keith Ball."

"Well," Jack begins. "Some of what I will tell you might shock you.

"You know how much I'm indebted to Uncle Keith. He has helped me with accommodation since I returned from India, and he has been helpful in other ways too. So don't think what I tell you is in any way a criticism of him.

"It all goes back to my father, who knew Uncle Keith from way back. My father was studying medicine at St. Thomas's Hospital and was on the brink of graduating when Uncle Keith asked him to do something so terrible I am finding it difficult to put into suitable words to tell you." Jack pauses.

"What did he ask your father to do?" asks Thomasine, intrigued.[4]

"He told him that he had a lady friend in high places who had unfortunately conceived a child out of wedlock with her lover." Jack pauses again and sighs.

"This grand lady knew that if her husband found out that she was bearing another man's child he would dispossess her and her other children and banish her from her home. She was distraught."

Jack mops his brow and continues: "Uncle Keith asked my father if he could perform an operation on the lady to…terminate…abort…the unborn baby."

Jack turns to Thomasine who is agog.

"The thought of conducting such a procedure was abhorrent to my father, not only because it was contrary to the whole meaning of the physicians' Hippocratic Oath which cherishes human life and upholds ethical standards against medical malfeasance, but also because it was against his own religious beliefs.

"But Uncle Keith was desperate to help the woman who was a patroness of certain charities Uncle Keith was helping. And then, when my father met her, he saw how completely devastated she was by her situation. So he complied with their wishes.

"He was taken one evening to a very big house in Mayfair and ushered into the lady's bedchamber where the heavy velvet curtains were drawn and only one, faithful, servant was present. My father carried out the procedure successfully, and the lady survived and was effusively grateful, but my father felt sick to the pit of his stomach, and never forgave himself." Jack pauses.

"Oh, Jack!" Thomasine exclaims. "That is, indeed, terrible."

"But that is not the end of the sorry matter," Jack continues. "A classmate of my father's at the hospital somehow got to hear about it. He was always jealous of my father's success in beating him in the exams, and he decided to pay him back by exposing his dreadful deed to the hospital authorities. My father was called before a committee to explain what he had done, and, as a result, he was barred from taking his final exams and banned from graduating in Medicine," Jack stops and turns to Thomasine who puts her hand on his.

"And so that was the end of my father's medical career, although he did complete his studies in pharmacy. Nevertheless, after he became a farmer, his medical knowledge stood him in good stead," Jack adds. "He looked after many of the poorer people in his village when they fell ill or broke bones or whatever. As I grew up on the farm he not only taught me a lot about farming, but also he taught me some medical skills, which were to come in useful.

"Do you remember that wedding in Wiltshire we all attended back in 1855? I was 14 at the time. Young James Price was getting married – his father was your uncle – your mother, Eliza's, and your aunt Mary's brother. Well. Uncle Keith was also there, with Mary Price, and when the wedding breakfast began, I suddenly saw him choking on a chicken bone. So I rushed over to him and banged him on his back and he coughed up the bone. He always says I saved his life – though anybody could have done what I did.

"As I said, Uncle Keith is extremely helpful to me – he says it's because I saved his life, but I suspect that he's still feeling guilty for being the cause of the end of my father's medical career."

"Keith shouldn't have asked your father to do such a thing," Thomasine concludes. "I'm surprised he had the gall to ask him."

"Well, to quote a cliché, it's no use crying over spilt milk," Jack says. "Nevertheless, that's how Uncle Keith, and many other people, operate their existence: by doing someone a favour and receiving a favour in return."

"Of course, Jack, I completely understand," Thomasine says, "I must go now, it's getting late and it's time for the children's tea. Shall we meet again here next Tuesday?"

Jack pauses, and then says with a hopeful smile: "I was wondering if you'd like to come with me to the latest exhibition at the Crystal Palace next Sunday – it's open now on Sundays – and would you like to bring your older children too?"

"That would be lovely," Thomasine agrees. "Will you come to my house and we'll go from there?"

Thomasine

As she walks back home, Thomasine mulls over what Jack has told her. *No man has ever talked about such things to me before,* she thinks. *Jack is starting to be a most interesting man.*

END NOTES CHAPTER 5

[1] This meeting is an oft-repeated family story, passed down through the generations.

[2] The store was renamed in the 1890s as Dickens & Jones.

[3] The first underground railway in the world, the Metropolitan Line, opened on 11 January 1863.

[4] Some of this comes from a letter (undated, courtesy Sue Mills).

6

The Crystal Palace

THE FOLLOWING SUNDAY morning, Jack arrives at Thomasine's front door, warmly dressed in an overcoat and a tweed cap. Nora, the maid, ushers him in, and Thomasine comes down the stairs with her two elder children and introduces them to Jack: Mary, aged seven, (usually called May) and Edward. The younger two, Roland and baby Herbert James (Bertie), are far too young to venture out in the cold weather. May and Edward are also warmly dressed in their new winter clothes, ready and eager for their expedition to the Crystal Palace,[1] the reincarnation of the original enormous glass and steel exhibition hall, now rebuilt at Sydenham in South London.

Turning to the two children, she says "We're going to Victoria Station by hansom cab and then we're taking the train to the Crystal Palace."

After reaching Victoria Station they set off in the train for Sydenham.

"There's lots to do out at Crystal Palace," Jack tells the children, "But I think you might find the dinosaur exhibition specially interesting."

May looks puzzled. "What's a dinosaur?"

"We'll see when we get there, But I'll let you into a secret now – dinosaurs are very, very old," replies Jack, smiling at the little girl who looks quite like her mother.

The two children have been on a train once before – when they travelled down to London from Yorkshire after the death of their father. Now, they excitedly look out the window as the train creaks and snorts its way out of London,

Jack turns to Thomasine.

"I'm glad we decided on this excursion," he says, "because I shan't see you for a fortnight after this. I have to go up to Scotland to help Uncle Keith with some problems concerning his properties in Edinburgh."

Remembering their last conversation at the teashop, Thomasine looks at Jack: "You do help Keith a great deal, don't you?"

"Yes," Jack replies. "I'm certainly indebted to him."

They reach the station at Crystal Palace and walk towards the great park where the enormous glass dome rears ahead of them.

The Crystal Palace

"I suggest we start by going to see the dog show – the children will enjoy it. Did they ever have a dog?" Jack asks.

"No, a dog in that damp, cold vicarage would simply have been an extra problem, but the children do love animals. Let's go and see the dog show!" Thomasine suggests.

Next, they come inside the vast main exhibition building and Thomasine marvels at the massive 4,500-pipe Great Organ which provides part of the music for the Crystal Palace orchestra. "It makes my little organ in the church at Devises seem miniscule, Fancy trying to play that beast!" Thomasine laughs. They wander through the fine art courts, the children marvelling at the displays of Egyptian mummies and the pharaohs' rich gold jewellery, and then the banquet halls in the Medieval court captivate them. "Look," Edward points out to May, "they didn't even have carpets in those days – just straw!".

"It's 11 o'clock already!" Jack exclaims after pulling out his fob watch. "How about a glass of lemonade, children?" They move out to the lemonade stand and all refresh themselves. Then, with the sun now shining, they wander around the spacious grounds until lunchtime, marvelling at the many fountains and cascades and the two extra-big fountains, spurting up water 250 feet (76 metres) high. By this time both children are thoroughly enjoying themselves, calling out "Uncle Jack, come and have a look at this!" and running about under the trees.

After lunch at the pie stall, Jack suggests they venture into the Maze, telling May and Edward that the Maze is a mysterious place full of hedges and pathways leading to dead ends, and with only one way out. "We'll all have to hold hands when we walk into the Maze so we don't get lost," he tells them. "Some people have got lost forever in the Maze!"

Fortunately, Jack manages to get a map of the Maze, but he insists they all hold hands from start to finish. The four of them set off and immediately take a wrong turning, ending up in a dead end. "Back we go to the start!" Jack instructs them. "This time we'll consult the map." Even with the map, it takes them at least an hour to negotiate the cleverly-constructed maze, planned by the famous landscape architect, Edward Milner, to entertain visitors to the Crystal Palace.

Sitting down on a park bench after their Maze adventure, Jack asks May and Edward if they'd like to go and see the tightrope-walking display next. The children agree enthusiastically but Edward asks: "When can we see the dinosaurs?"

"First, we'll go and watch the tightrope walker, and then we'll end up at the Dinosaur court," Jack reassures him.

Thomasine finds herself relaxing for the first time in ages. *Jack's getting on so well with May and Edward! He seems to have a special knack with children – indeed with everyone,* she muses.

After watching, wide-eyed, the death-defying antics of the tightrope walker, they move on to the Dinosaur Court. "Dinosaurs," Jack explains to the children as they lean over the railing and gaze at the plaster models of huge creatures in front of them, "are animals like giant lizards which lived millions of years ago. So you won't actually see live dinosaurs – these are just models of them. But when you look at them you'll see they look like enormous birds. That's because dinosaurs are the ancestors of birds."

Thomasine looks at Jack in amazement. "But, Jack, how could these creatures have lived on Earth millions of years ago when the Earth is only 4,000 years old?"

Jack looks at Thomasine gently. "Tommy," he says. "The Church is still taking its time to understand what Charles Darwin's Theory of Evolution is about. You wouldn't, as a vicar's wife, have heard much about Darwin's theory We'll have a long talk about it another day."

By now, the late afternoon sun is setting and it's time to walk to the station to catch the train back to Victoria Station. Young Edward is looking very tired and Jack picks him up and carries him as they walk.

"They've certainly had a big day," Thomasine says. "Jack, you've given them a lot of fun. Life hasn't been very much fun for them lately. They still miss their father."

As they reach the station they see a very long queue ahead of them. "It's hard to realise that around 14,000 people a day visit the Crystal Palace – the grounds are so spacious, you only see the crowds at the railway station" Jack says.

Finally, they manage to climb onto a train and settle down in their seats. Both children are sleepy and soon doze off. Thomasine and Jack talk quietly, reminiscing about old times at Stoke Prior. Soon Thomasine, too, finds herself nodding off.

"Lean your head on my shoulder," says Jack, and they travel on comfortably.

"Tickets please!" the ticket inspector calls out, progressing along the carriage just before they reach Victoria Station. As he clips Jack's tickets, the inspector looks at the drowsy trio sitting with him.

"You've a bonny family there, sir," he says. "They look as if they've had a good time at the Palace."

Jack nods and smiles.

When they reach Thomasine's house, the nanny is waiting in the hallway and takes the sleepy children upstairs.

Jack turns to Thomasine and pulls her to him.

"Tommy, darling," he says, and kisses her gently and passionately. Thomasine feels a thrill coursing through her whole body; she has never been kissed quite like this before.

Jack strokes her cheek.

"Goodbye, Tommy, I'll see you in two weeks' time."

****

Over the next fortnight while Jack is away in Scotland, the memory of Jack's kiss keeps on returning to Thomasine as she goes about her daily routine, checking the day's menus with the cook, having breakfast and lunch with the children, and generally keeping her household running smoothly. She's not used to having so many servants, and, in a way, she misses the hard work she did back in Yorkshire, coping with the vicissitudes of the damp vicarage.

I must admit I'm missing Jack, she thinks, as she goes about her day, recalling their happy excursion to the Crystal Palace, and how the two children enjoyed Jack's sense of fun. And then, that kiss...

This is ridiculous, Thomasine chides herself. *Here I am, a grown woman, mother of my four surviving children, still in mourning for my dear husband and my dear Father and brother. I'm behaving like a silly young girl.*

Nevertheless she is yearning to see Jack again, and she counts the days to their next meeting at the teashop. On the allotted Tuesday at 3 o'clock, she walks down to the teashop through the puddles and slush of a cold November day. The lamplights are glowing as she pushes open the door and is greeted by the waitress, now treating her as a regular customer, who ushers her to the window seat where Jack is sitting, smiling eagerly at the sight of her.

"Darling Tommy," he greets her, giving her a chaste peck on the cheek. "Come and sit down and tell me what's been happening since I went away. How are the children? Did they get a good night's sleep after our outing?" After some general chatter, Jack pulls out a letter from his pocket.

"I seem to be Uncle Keith's postman," he says, alluding to that earlier, dire, letter he had delivered to Thomasine. "But this time, Uncle Keith is wishing you a happy Christmas – he's stuck up in Scotland and embroiled in a nasty legal battle over one of his properties, a warehouse in Glasgow, and he can't get back to London until the matter is resolved, and that won't be until after Christmas."

Thomasine opens the letter and scans it quickly. "My Dearest Thomasine," it begins, and then Sir William Keith describes the difficulties he is encountering in Glasgow. The letter goes on to relate how Jack has been a great help, looking after his other business in Edinburgh, while he grappled with the court case. "I have given Jack some finance to cover the cost of a hearty Christmas dinner for you and the children," Sir Keith adds. "I'm sure Jack will take care of you in place of me."

Jack, acutely aware of the delicacy of the matter, looks searchingly into Thomasine's eyes.

"Tommy, how do you feel about this? I don't want to transgress Sir Keith's trust, after all, he is affianced to you [2] – but I'd dearly love to spend Christmas Day with you and your family!"

Thomasine smiles: "Yes, Jack, I would love you to come to Christmas dinner – and the children would be delighted too. After all, it is Keith's idea."

Relieved at Thomasine's response, Jack relaxes, and they drink their tea in quiet contemplation before Thomasine suggests that perhaps Jack should come and visit a few times before Christmas so that he and the children can get to know each other better.

And so a pattern begins. Thomasine and Jack still meet at the teashop every Tuesday and talk and talk, and on several Sundays Jack comes to her house where he visits the children in the nursery, getting to know young Roland and baby Herbert (Bertie), and playing magic tricks with May and Edward. "Uncle Jack" soon becomes a good friend. After the children are put to bed, Jack and Thomasine retire to the drawing room where she plays the piano and he sings, his mellow tenor surprising her with its range and sensitivity. *He is certainly a very attractive man,* Thomasine can't help thinking again as he stands beside the piano, the lamplight shining down on to his light brown, almost golden hair.

Jack doesn't attempt to kiss her again, and Thomasine, acknowledging the sensitivity of the situation, appreciates his forbearance – although deep down, she'd dearly love him to embrace her again.

On one of their Tuesday meetings at the teashop, Thomasine probes Jack on his life in India and he tells her about camp life where he was mainly in charge of the horses. "It was a pretty humdrum experience much of the time, although we did get involved in a few skirmishes. I become friends with some interesting people here and there. Although I was just a member of the ranks, I got to know some of the officers through my work with their horses.

"And," he adds, "I became romantically involved with one of the officers' wives, even though I was a lowly "rough rider". She was in her late 30s and I was only 21. We were very close for a time. She was quite notorious for her penchant for younger men, and our little affair didn't seem to worry her husband in the slightest – indeed, he was busy flirting with other officers' wives. Officers in the British Army in India enjoy a very pampered existence – when they aren't fighting. I must confess my lady friend was very happy to educate me in the finer things in life. And I'm grateful for what I learned. She was a lovely woman," a wistful expression flits through his eyes.

Some of his stories about Army life make Thomasine laugh out loud. She hasn't laughed much since the death of her husband, but with Jack, the old, lively Thomasine returns.

Listening to his reminiscences, Thomasine realises that Jack has enjoyed a wealth of experiences since she had known him back at Stoke Prior.

END NOTES CHAPTER 6

[1] The Crystal Palace, the brainchild of Prince Albert, was an enormous, dazzling glass-and-steel structure erected in London's Hyde Park for the Great Exhibition of 1851. After the Exhibition closed, the Crystal Palace was relocated to Penge Common, Sydenham, South London, where Queen Victoria opened it in 1854. The new Crystal Palace featured a new glass dome, along with elaborate additions and courts, all set in spacious grounds designed by Edward Milner, featuring waterfalls and fountains, a maze, and other attractions for the crowds who visited it until its destruction by fire in 1936

[2] *Two Families, op cit.*, p.9.

7

A Christmas Vow

CHRISTMAS DAY approaches. Prince Albert, the late consort to Queen Victoria, had achieved some major reforms during his short life (he died in 1861 of pneumonia, aged only 47). He had worked to abolish slavery worldwide, had modernised the Royal household and estates, championed educational reform and helped initiate the Great Exhibition in the Crystal Palace in 1851, among other achievements. But for many people, especially children, his greatest reform had been to revolutionise Christmas in England, popularising the German tradition of the Christmas tree and introducing a hearty Christmas dinner and other amusements to what had previously been a somewhat muted English festival.

As she helps the children to decorate the little tree in the drawing room on Christmas Eve, and plans with Cook a menu of turkey and mince pies, Thomasine, looking back to the rather perfunctory yuletide celebrations of her childhood, blesses Prince Albert's memory.

On Christmas morning she wakes up and looks into her wardrobe and makes a big decision: *I'm going to put away my widow's weeds today – for ever. I will never forget dear James; a kinder husband would be hard to find. And poor little Amelia, I shall never forget that gentle child. Nor will I ever forget my dear Father and my dear brother. They didn't deserve their dreadful fate. But life must go on – and it's Christmas. And Jack will be coming to Christmas dinner!*

After breakfast, Thomasine takes out her navy-blue-and-white best dress, her red overcoat, a smart red felt bonnet and her best boots, and gets ready to take the children to the local church for the Christmas service. It is a cold, clear day with a little rain hovering on the horizon, but no sign of snow – London hasn't had a white Christmas for at least ten years. The rest of the morning and early afternoon is spent on the now traditional Christmas activities – opening presents and playing games. May opens Thomasine's gift to her to find a copy of Charles Kingsley's just-published *Water Babies*, while Edward gets a wooden railway engine on wheels. Three-year-old Roland clutches a toy rabbit as he chases the older children around the house. Baby Herbert James is still too young to know what Christmas is about.

"When is Uncle Jack coming?" asks May with a note of anticipation in her voice.

"At 4 o'clock," says Thomasine, feeling a sense of anticipation herself.

On the dot of four Jack arrives, bearing gifts for the children. He gives Thomasine a big hug and then turns to May and Edward who have rushed into the hallway to greet him.

"Come into the drawing room, the fire will warm you up," Thomasine says, and they all go in to sit by the tree.

Jack calls Edward over. "Edward, you remember our trip to the Crystal Palace? Well, open this present and you'll think you're back there."

Edward unwraps his gift to find a big box decorated with a map of the world with the name "THE CRYSTAL PALACE GAME" printed across it. Inside is a game which takes players on a voyage around the world to far-off places, teaching them geography and history on the way.

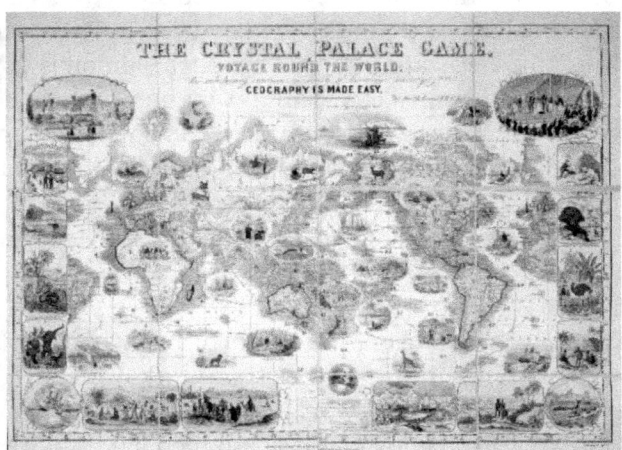

The Crystal Palace Game – British Library Collection

Next, Jack hands May a smaller package. Inside is a wooden string puppet which May immediately starts "walking" across the carpet. Jack then gives Roland a toy monkey which squeaks when you press it. And for baby Bertie, there's a rattle.

With the children immersed in their Christmas gifts, Jack turns to Thomasine, who is now wearing a soft pale blue dress and a colourful flower-patterned shawl. "You look absolutely lovely," Jack says, admiring her shining dark hair and sparkling eyes. "I haven't seen you look so happy and well. No more black!"

"No," replies Thomasine, smiling at Jack "I think I'm starting to come alive again."

At 6.30 pm they all sit down to Christmas dinner in the dining room where Thomasine has decorated the table with sprigs of holly, and placed candles in the centre to give out a softer light than the oil lamps. Jack opens a box he has brought and pulls out a handful of brightly-coloured paper bon-bons, giving one to Thomasine and two to May and Edward. "I haven't forgotten you, Roland," he says, observing the look on the little boy's face. "You'll have your own one in a minute after I've shared mine with your mother."

The children haven't seen crackers before and are puzzled. "These bon bons will give you a bit of a surprise when you pull them," Jack explains. "They were invented a few years ago by a confectioner called Tom Smith who had been to Paris where he noticed that the Parisians wrapped up sugar almonds in bright paper, called 'bon bons'. Tom Smith went home to London and then worked out a way to wrap up lollies in coloured paper and insert a strip wick into them, so when you pulled the cracker it would pop-crack!

"Here, May, you hold this end of the bon bon and ask Edward to hold the other end. Now!" And sure enough, the cracker pops.

After all the crackers are popped and paper party hats donned, Cook brings in an enormous roast turkey, roast potatoes, and gravy, peas and carrots. The feast concludes with mince pies and custard, and the happy children are then led upstairs to bed by Nanny, who is carrying a little basket that Thomasine has packed with a plate of mince pies and custard and a little bottle of brandy so Nanny can sit in front of her fire in her room and doze off peacefully.

While Cook clears the table and tidies the kitchen before retiring to her room for her own nip of brandy, Thomasine and Jack go back into the drawing room where Jack pours them both a glass of champagne and they sit down together on the sofa in front of the fire.

"This is the best Christmas I've ever had," Jack says, "especially because I'm having it with you." And he puts his arm around Thomasine as they sip their champagne. Thomasine takes his hand for a moment and leans closer to him. "Jack," she murmurs, "You gave the children so much fun. They really love your presents!"

"Well," Jack says, taking a small parcel out of his pocket, and handing it to Thomasine. "I hope you'll enjoy your present too."

Thomasine unwraps the gift and discovers inside a small box. Opening it, she finds a simple gold chain with a pure ruby hanging from it.

"Let me put it on you, Tommy," says Jack, gently placing it around her neck. "I bought this gold chain and ruby in India a few years ago and vowed to keep it until I found someone I really cared for. And that is you." Then Jack kisses Thomasine softly at first, and, as she responds, more passionately. After a long while, they pause and look at one another.

"Tommy, darling, I love you," says Jack.

"And I love you too," Thomasine replies.

"Tommy, I'd like to carry you off to my bed and make love to you forever," Jack almost groans. "But what are we going to do about this? Here I am, desperately in love with the fiancée of my good friend and benefactor, but I can't help it. I know I can't live without you, but I'm not being fair to you."

"Jack, darling," Thomasine says, sitting upright and looking at him. "I think it's time we had a good talk about everything. We can't go on drifting along any longer, both feeling the way we do."

Thankful that Thomasine feels as he does – and has the good sense to want to discuss it – Jack pours each of them another glass of champagne and settles back on the sofa next to her. The house is quiet, and the only sound is the crackling firewood in the grate. Outside, the wind is swirling around the house and the gas street lamps are spluttering.

"Tommy," Jack begins. "What I'm going to say now is very important and serious, but I think it is time to say it. I would very dearly love to marry you."

Thomasine's eyes widen.

"Now don't say anything yet," Jack goes on. "I want you to know that I will understand completely, although I will be overwhelmed with grief, if you say you can't agree to this. I realise you have four young children, and that if you marry Uncle Keith you will become Lady Ball and will live a comfortable life ever after. Your children won't lack for a good education and a privileged start in life, and Uncle Keith will always look after you.

"I also realise that at present I don't have any occupation. But I'm sure I will find something to do soon which will bring in a sufficient income to keep us all off the street. But above all, I want to marry and cherish you for the rest of my life."

Thomasine sits silently for a time. There is much to absorb, although some of these matters have been churning through her mind too. *I would be taking an enormous risk,* she thinks. *But I definitely do love Jack.* She rouses herself from her reverie and turns to Jack:

"Jack, you'll have to give me time to think about all this. It's a very big decision to make – and I have to think of the children. If it was just me, alone, I'd accept your offer immediately. I most certainly do love you very much."

Jack puts his arm around her again and pulls her close to him. "I understand completely, Tommy," he says. "You must think very carefully. Take your time. If you decide to say 'yes' I will need to confess the whole matter to Uncle Keith. I cannot do or say anything further until I have come clean with him. It would be deceitful to do otherwise.

"Uncle Keith will be returning in five days' time – next Wednesday. I would need to tell him as soon as he gets back. Could you let me know your decision by then?"

Thomasine nods in silent agreement and Jack embraces her, giving her another passionate kiss. Then he gets up:

"I must leave now – before my desire gets the better of my manners!" he says.

"Oh," exclaims Thomasine, "I've forgotten to give you your Christmas present. Here it is, it's a diary – not a very exciting gift. I'm afraid,"

Opening his gift, Jack looks at the handsome, leather-bound diary. "I hope I will chart the first year of our life together in this diary," he says.[1]

"Goodbye, my darling Jack," Thomasine says. "I'll have a good think about everything, and I'll send you a little note in a day or two, telling you what I have decided. But you must know I do love you dearly."

With that, Jack goes to the front door and lets himself out. He goes back to Uncle Keith's house through a thick London fog, walking quickly along deserted streets before reaching Leinster Gardens.

END NOTE CHAPTER 7

[1] Sadly, this diary has been lost – apart from one memorable entry, which we will see later.

8

Events Move Quickly

OVER THE NEXT couple of days Thomasine debates in her mind the pros and cons of giving up a secure home and future for herself and the children for marriage to Jack. It is a case of common sense versus rash romanticism, she knows. *Yet Keith, although fond of me, would not be a husband in the true sense – he wouldn't share the marital bed – he isn't that way inclined. Nor would he be at my side much of the time because of his widespread interests.*

Whereas Jack is arousing in her feelings she has never experienced before. He excites her. And, yes, he has already demonstrated how well he gets on with her children. "Uncle Jack" was now, to them, part of the family. And he is clever and strong and capable. *It wasn't his fault that he had given up the Army – he was bright enough to realise he had no future there. He's bound to find suitable employment soon. We're both young. Why not start a new life together?*

And, Thomasine has to admit to herself, *I would be free of my long obligation to Keith. I would be a person in my own right, not dependent on him. All my life I have felt grateful to Keith. But now I want to be independent of him, to make my own decisions and run my own life.*

I will marry Jack, she finally decides, and on the Tuesday summons a messenger boy to take a note addressed to Jack to Keith's house in Leinster Gardens.

Jack sends back a note saying:

> "Darling Tommy! I will tell Uncle Keith on his return. He will no doubt ask to see you to ascertain your thoughts on the matter. Until then, I live in hope and joy at your decision. My deep love, Jack".

Sir William Keith Ball does indeed want to see Thomasine on his return that Wednesday, and he sends a note inviting her to afternoon tea that day. Thomasine, feeling somewhat nervous, arrives at the Leinster Gardens house, and is ushered into his study by a maid.

"My dear Thomasine," Keith says, getting up from his desk and giving her a hug. Pointing to two leather armchairs, he guides her to sit down. "Come and tell me all about it."

A maid brings in tea and they sit opposite each other in the two armchairs

Thomasine hesitantly tells Keith that she has become very fond of Jack and that she is inclined to accept his proposal of marriage. She thanks Keith for his own offer of marriage, which, she says, is an offer of a privileged life which no woman would be inclined to forgo. But, she adds, she has, to her own surprise, fallen in love with Jack.

To her relief, Keith treats the whole matter with his habitual urbanity and gentle humour.

"My dear Thomasine!" he smiles. "I let you out of my sight for a month and you run off with another man! Tut, tut. Now I must offer you some advice in this matter before you make a final decision. Were you to marry me, you would become Lady Ball and you would be afforded all the perks and privileges that go with that station in life. You would have your own personal maid and your own income to buy clothes and other items. You would be invited with me to attend dinner parties where you would meet very important people – the highest in the land. And I know you would grace those tables with your elegance and wit.

"Your children would receive the best care and education, and none of you would ever need for anything. I know Jack is a fine young man – but what can he offer compared to that?"

Thomasine leans forward across the tea table and clutches Keith's hand. "Keith," she says. "You have always looked after me and I'm deeply grateful for all you have done for me. I love you dearly, but not in the same way that I love Jack. I must follow my heart – mad though it might seem."

Sir Keith smiles "Then, Thomasine, you have my blessing. I must say I'm not really surprised. Jack is a very attractive and good young man. The two of you will make a fine couple."

****

Events move quickly from that point. Thomasine and Jack became officially engaged, and a wedding date, April 14th, is set. The children react favourably to the news and Jack spends more and more time with them at Thomasine's house (which Sir Keith continues to make available to her until her marriage).

An old schoolfriend of Jack's, who has moved to the country, lends his London flat in Pimlico for Jack and Thomasine to frequent discreetly for some privacy together until their wedding. It is an idyllic time for them both. Jack also starts work on a new job in an auction house, learning how to value silver and furniture. He shows aptitude as an auctioneer and is getting on well with the other staff. He is also working with Uncle Keith on some of his multifarious business projects.

"It's about time I introduced you to my parents," Jack tells Thomasine. "I think you will like them – and they will like you, once they get over the fact that I'm about to marry a widow with four children!"

On the train to Wiltshire where Jack's parents live on their farm at Pewsey, Jack tells Thomasine more about them.

"As you will recall, my father was close to graduating as a doctor when that unfortunate incident concerning Uncle Keith occurred. Well, after that, my father turned to farming, and he was quite successful, even though he was never rich. Despite this, he has been presented to Queen Victoria. He taught me quite a lot of medical skills, which were to come in handy when I joined the Army. He looked after the poor in our district.

"I'm the second eldest of 11 children, four boys and seven girls. We children were not brought up as snobs. We were all taught to behave as gentlemen and gentle ladies in the best meaning of the word[1]

"Tell me about your mother," Thomasine interrupts.

"Her maiden name was Mary Anne Yeats and her father, John Samuel Yeats RN, was a friend of Uncle Keith's" Jack says. "The Yeats are navy people and I seem to recall that they knew Uncle Keith through his father, the Admiral. Anyway, Uncle Keith introduced John Samuel Yeats's daughter, Mary Anne, to my father and they married, which is why I'm here."

"Keith certainly weaves a tangled web!" Thomasine laughs.

The meeting with Jack's parents proves a success – after a brief hesitation over the fact that the bride-to-be is four years older than their son and has four young children – and the parents give her their blessing, and send their daughter, Phoebe Alice, to the wedding.

The ceremony takes place, as planned, on April 14th 1864, at St Philip Church, Dalston, Middlesex. Thomasine, in a simple cream gown, stands at the altar and glances at Jack. He looks back at her, his slightly-drooping, humorous eyes shining. *Well, Thomasine thinks, life's not going to be dull with this man!* Witnesses to the marriage are Phoebe Alice, and Lucy Tucker, a cousin of Jack's and a favourite of Sir Keith's. Another guest is Jack's aunt Louisa, his mother's 35-year-old youngest sister. At the reception Thomasine notes that Keith, who is present as an honoured guest, is paying Louisa particular attention. "Perhaps Louisa will become Keith's new 'damsel in distress'," she jokes to Jack, and subsequent events are to prove her intuition correct.

St Philip Church of England, Dalston, Middlesex where Thomasine and Jack marry on April 14th 1864.

After the wedding, Thomasine and Jack take a brief honeymoon in Wales, leaving the children in the care of their Nanny. (Thomasine's Cooper children will retain their surname Cooper.)

59

Thomasine still has some relatives in Wales and she declares "we are Welsh on both sides. I always say I am Welsh to the backbone, and proud of my forefathers, especially my dear Father."[2] and she buys a Welsh cloak which she sometimes wears for the rest of her life.[3]

On their return to London, Thomasine and Jack have to knuckle down to reality, leasing from Uncle Keith a smaller house in Bayswater which they can just afford on Jack's auctioneer's salary, and they are reduced to having only a maid – no cook or nanny. Thomasine makes the children's summer clothes on the new Chadwick & Jones sewing machine[4] which Sir William Keith gave them as a wedding present, and she copes gamely with all the household chores. But Jack is concerned:

"Tommy, this isn't the kind of life you deserve. You gave up a great deal to marry me. Now I must do something to justify your trust."

He has been contemplating broaching the subject of emigrating to the Colonies. Would Thomasine be prepared to start a new life in New Zealand? After all, her mother and brother, Henry, are there, and most of her younger siblings. But Thomasine bridles at the idea.

"I couldn't go there – after what those Maoris did to my Father and brother! I know my mother and my other sisters and brothers are there, and they seem to like life in New Zealand,, but no, Jack, I simply couldn't face it. And anyway, the Maori Wars are still being waged out there."

Jack perseveres in his desire to emigrate and he discovers a possible solution: The American Civil War of 1861 has left the English cotton industry floundering from a collapse of cotton supplies from the American southern states, which has caused a "cotton famine" in England. Many of the cotton mills in Lancashire and other parts of North-West England have stopped rolling and thousands of workers have lost their jobs. British millers have looked round for alternative supplies of cotton, and latched on to Australia as a promising source. The fledgling Queensland Government[5] has begun to offer financial incentives to encourage English people to emigrate and set up cotton plantations. Jack's ears prick up at this and he puts the idea to

Thomasine, who favours the idea of emigrating to Australia; she dreads another winter in England with her children vulnerable to bronchitis and other winter ills. And she knows Jack, having lived so long in India, is starting to have itchy feet.

"Yes, Jack!" she finally decides, "Let's give Australia a go! Uncle Keith is bound to help us with some finance."[6]

Thomasine starts to get the children accustomed to the idea of emigrating to Australia by playing Edward's Christmas present of the Crystal Palace Game with them. It provides useful information about Australia which they can absorb while having fun with the game.

With his customary verve, Jack decides they shouldn't stint themselves on the voyage. Their request for further financial help from Sir Keith being rebuffed, they use £800 from Thomasine's late husband Edward James Cooper's probate settlement (the rest of that £1500 pension is never again touched by Thomasine or Jack[7]), and they book Saloon Class (First Class) passages for themselves and the four children aboard the 1346-ton Black Ball Line's *Queen of the Colonies*, under Captain Henry Jones.

They set off in late June 1864 to board the *Queen of the Colonies* and arrive at the quay at Gravesend, climb the gangplank of the handsome sailing ship, and are shown to their cabins. The children are, naturally, ebullient and start racing around their quarters and back up on deck. Meanwhile, Thomasine and Jack settle into their relatively spacious cabin and look at one another with a sense of achievement mingled with anxiety; it will be a long and possibly perilous voyage ahead.

But their expectations of departing England are thwarted for almost a week while their ship lingers in the dock awaiting some late passengers, as Thomasine recounts in a letter to her brother William. While waiting for their ship to sail, Thomasine also voices in her letter her assessment of Keith's new attitude.

She refers to Keith not being helpful with financial assistance. No doubt Sir William has decided that enough is enough; he had bent over backwards to provide financial support for Thomasine, despite her decision not to marry him. He probably feels that it is now up to Jack to take on full responsibility for his wife and her children.

"The Queen of the Colonies"
Gravesend[8]

My Dearest William,
Jack and I and the children are on board our ship and expect to sail to Brisbane on Saturday. We hope for a safe voyage and that you will soon follow us and come and help us if you can or at any rate come out to us and see what is to be done

Sir William turned disagreeable and did not do half or a quarter what he promised at the last, but we hope to get on nevertheless. I cannot afford to let you have any more money than I have at present dear Willie or I gladly would to help you out but we are very short ourselves. Sir William [Keith] will try and stop you coming to us if he can but never heed him, say you intend to go to Brisbane on your own account and take the first situation you can get. ...

Jack is willing and anxious that you should join him; I am sure you will like each other. We came on board last

Saturday and are detained here waiting for some passengers from Scotland and shall be here I expect a week in all. I can't write much as I have but one hand at liberty as Bertie is on my lap and has helped to grease and . . . this letter. Try and save all the money you can to come out to us and make a good beginning for yourself. I take it for granted that your Captain will let you off, I sent £16 to the Paymaster of your ship, £13 of it to buy your discharge and £3 for your self, if he will not let you off you must take the money to help you out to Brisbane.

If you think it best you might as well go and see Sir William [Keith] and see if he will help you or has any message to send to us. We don't know what Jack will do when he gets out to Brisbane as he thinks he cannot begin to farm for himself as Sir William has not let us have enough money so he will most likely take a situation of some kind at first. We are very well and all send our love and lots of kisses to Uncle Willie...
love, your own affectionate loving sister. Thomasine Browne.[9]

Thomasine

The ship departs Gravesend (about 23 miles from central London) on July 3rd at about 4 pm with 442 passengers and 1000 tons of cargo on board.

END NOTES CHAPTER 8

[1] The Browne family pedigree, courtesy Sue Mills.

[2] *The Two Families op cit.*

[3] This garment is on display at the Gold Coast Hinterland Heritage Museum, Mudgeeraba, Queensland.

[4] Cost about £6.

[5] Queensland was declared a State, independent of New South Wales, in 1859.

[6] Thomasine is soon to be disabused of this hope – see her letter to her brother, William (footnote 8).

[7] The rest of James Cooper's pension was passed on to the Cooper children when they came of age.

[8] Letter from Thomasine to her brother, William, written during the week before they sailed on July 3rd, 1864.

[9] William decided not to take up Thomasine's offer and instead went to Canada where he married Susannah Cruse, born in 1844 in Lamaline, Newfoundland. She died in 1895 in Dartmouth, Nova Scotia.

9

To a New Life

AS *QUEEN OF THE COLONIES* unfurls her sails in the English Channel, Thomasine and Jack lean over the rail and watch England slowly disappear.

"Darling Tommy!" Jack exclaims. "We're off to a new life! We will have to work hard when we get to Australia, but I vow we'll never lack for anything and we'll enjoy good food and companionship!"

Thomasine is equally optimistic. For a lady of her class in those days she has made a big decision, but she isn't regretting it, although at times she frets privately over the children's future. It is a big step.

By opting for Saloon Class, they enjoy a far more pleasurable voyage than that which Thomasine's parents Michael and Eliza and their family suffered when they travelled to New Zealand aboard the *Nourmahal* five years previously. The Saloon Class food is even quite palatable because the ship carries a live larder of pigs and poultry which are slaughtered during the voyage to provide tasty and nutritious meals for the more privileged passengers. The cows on board provide fresh milk, and the only food these privileged passengers crave is fresh fruit. The wine on board, shared by the ship's officers, flows, and Thomasine and Jack join in the regular concerts held for Saloon Class passengers where Thomasine plays the piano and Jack and other passengers sing. The children make friends with other Saloon Deck children and play deck quoits and start to have the run of the ship.

One evening Jack has been carousing with some of the officers and fellow passengers and they have all drunk far too much. Later, back in his cabin, a still-inebriated Jack bemoans in his diary: "Pardo and I got drunk tonight. Tommy said she won't sleep with me tonight. Whatever shall I do?"[1]

But this is not to say there aren't bad days too, when the *Queen of the Colonies* hits rough weather and the waves break over the deck and in through the portholes into the first class cabins, not to mention below decks where the waves engulf those in Steerage. Sometimes the seas become so rough the passengers have to be tied to their chairs, or they simply remain in bed in their cabins while the storm rages.

On the plus side, however, the voyage is singularly disease-free, with few cases of serious illness or other medical emergencies for the ship's doctor, Mr. J.H.P. Oldmeadow, who copes with one birth and only one passenger death (that of an 18-month-old infant named Ellen Hill, who has suffered extreme dehydration after repeated attacks of diarrhoea).[2] There is also one crew death: on July 24th one of the ordinary seamen, who has washed his clothes in rainwater on deck, climbs the rigging to dry them, falls from the rigging and is drowned.[2]

The run from Cape Horn to Australia is pushed by the howling Roaring Forties, bowling *Queen of the Colonies* along at a furious pace, and the voyage notches up a record for the trip from England to Australia of only 75 days,

Advertisement for the Queen of the Colonies

A report of the voyage in the *Brisbane Courier* the following day[3] paints a glowing picture of conditions on board *Queen of the Colonies* – in stark contrast to the findings of a Queensland Government Select Committee the previous year which found that conditions endured by Black Ball Line passengers, particularly in Steerage Class, in previous years were horrendous. Squalid conditions prevailed, with typhoid and other deadly diseases rampant and living conditions not merely squalid but disgusting.[4] Many of the ships had no lavatory facilities in steerage where up to 500 passengers lived below deck, cooking and sleeping in ill-lit, cramped quarters. The cabin class passengers too, did not escape the condemnation of the Select Committee which, it alleged were the cause of immorality and bad behaviour on board. They brought alcohol on board and sold it to the steerage passengers and took part in "immoral activities" with the female steerage passengers.

But by the following year, when Thomasine and Jack and family board the *Queen of the Colonies*, the Black Ball Line, (which has had more-or-less a monopoly on emigration shipping, apart from a few government-run ships) has pulled up its socks and done much to improve conditions on its ships, as the *Brisbane Courier* reports. "…the government doctor sent to inspect the ship – the *Queen of the Colonies* – on its arrival, Dr Hobbs, speaks in the highest terms of the orderly and clean appearance of the ship, and informs us that the passengers seem to be of a stamp somewhat above the average of those who have recently arrived." And at a meeting on arrival of the ship's passengers held in the Brisbane School of Arts, the newspaper reports "a chronometer was presented to Captain Jones in appreciation of his care and watchfulness during the voyage. One second-cabin passenger expresses thanks to the Black Ball Line for the manner in which the arrangements for their comfort, health and morality had been carried out, and adds that the provisions served to cabin passengers had been excellent and far above the quality normally found on board ship. Passengers state that they had been blessed with a "good ship, a good captain and a good doctor," for all of which they are "certainly indebted to the Black Ball Line."

Having arrived at Moreton Bay, located about eight-and-three-quarter miles (14 kilometres) from Brisbane, around 4 pm on Thursday 22nd September, Thomasine, Jack, and family, along with some of the other First Cabin passengers, are taken off the ship that evening in a small steam boat, the *Nowra,* and are transported to Brisbane and booked into a central hotel for the night. Because it is dark and the city is barely lighted, (though the Brisbane Gas company has been incorporated recently and gas lights are on their way) they have to wait until morning to peer out of their hotel windows and see what Brisbane looks like.

What they do see on awakening next morning comes as a surprise. They have never seen a city so tiny before, nor a city built mainly from wood. The city they start exploring is in many ways a primitive frontier town, similar to towns in the American Wild West, with unpaved and unlit streets and a poor water supply. At that time, the municipality of Brisbane contains only about 20,000 people, while the population of the whole of the newly-constituted Colony of Queensland[5] is around the 62,000 mark. Even in the main street, Princes Street, and the other central streets, the buildings are mainly of wood, while in the back streets there is a straggle of pubs, bars and bordellos, catering to the tastes of visiting timber cutters and sailors

"I suddenly feel like a real pioneer!" Jack exclaims after they start to find out more about the Colony and its capital.

****

Jack learns quite a lot about Brisbane from their hotel proprietor, who prides himself on his grasp of history. He tells Jack that the area around Brisbane has been inhabited for tens of thousands of years by Aboriginal tribes, principally the Yugambeh. The first European to explore the area was Matthew Flinders who reached Moreton Bay in 1799, but he was unable to locate what later became known as the Brisbane River, perhaps because it was hidden by sandbanks at that time. It was a further 26 years before any Europeans settled permanently in the area after the colony of New South Wales decided to offload some of its worst convicts to a new penal settlement in Moreton Bay at Redcliffe Point. Meanwhile, surveyor John Oxley was persevering in his exploration of the Brisbane River, which he had discovered in 1823, and in 1825 the penal colony was moved from Moreton Bay to a peninsula on the Brisbane River, where it was still called the "Moreton Bay" penal settlement until the fledgling city of Brisbane was officially named after the

Governor of New South Wales, Sir Thomas Brisbane, who had visited the area in 1824.

Many thousands of convicts were imprisoned there, suffering extremely harsh conditions. Quite a few escaped, some managing to survive in the harsh bushland south of the colony. Some were helped by Aborigines, and a few managed to set up settlements on the northern rivers of New South Wales. The Aborigines did not welcome the penal colony and tried to starve it out by setting fire to its corn fields. The tribes involved suffered the ire of the penal authorities and many Aborigines were shot and killed in a series of early confrontations.

By the 1830s the British Government had begun to question the viability of the Brisbane penal colony; its numbers were dropping, and Australia's abundance of agricultural products – and thus, farming jobs – was beginning to attract more and more British migrants. In 1838, the area was opened up for free settlers, as distinct from convicts.

By 1839 the Moreton Bay area was officially surveyed and from then on free settlers arrived to take advantage of the abundance of timber in local forests. Once cleared, land was used for grazing and other farming activities, and the penal colony eventually closed.

In 1859 the Municipality of Brisbane was proclaimed, and Queensland was formally established as a self-governing colony of Great Britain, separate from New South Wales.

END NOTES CHAPTER 9

[1] This is the only extant quote from Jack's long-lost diary.

[2] There is no report of a rescue being attempted. To stop a ship of that size in full sail would have been a difficult task, by which time the unfortunate sailor would most probably have drowned.

[3] Report of the voyage in *The Brisbane Courier* Friday 23rd September 1864.

[4] In 1863 a select committee was appointed by the Queensland Parliament to enquire into and report on the operation and working of the immigration laws. The Select Committee also pinpointed the cabin passengers who, it was alleged, were the cause of immorality and bad behaviour on board.

Thomasine

[5] Queensland was declared a separate State from New South Wales in 1859.

10

Fire!

AFTER A WEEK staying at their hotel in Queen Street, where Thomasine and Jack spend much of their time enjoying the comfort of the big bed in their room, and where their first child is conceived, they decide they must conserve their money, and so move away from the centre of the city to a small guesthouse.

They then spend two months coming to grips with Queensland and negotiating their future plans. Jack, by nature gregarious, makes friends in the local pubs and around the town and begins to form a picture of the opportunities available. We do not know exactly what happens next, for Thomasine remains tight-lipped about a bad experience they seem to have had. All she ever says about what has happened is in a letter to her brother William in which she says: "*If you come here you must make up your mind to a bush life as it is ruin to live in Brisbane.*"[1] But they seem to have lost a good deal of money, perhaps in some false scheme offered to them as newcomers by a confidence trickster.

This hastens their plan to start farming, in particular, to grow cotton. Jack learns that quite a few settlers are doing well down on the Northern rivers of New South Wales and he contemplates a move there, but then he becomes interested in the rich agricultural promise of the area south of Brisbane which has just begun to be surveyed, and they apply for some land on the Barrow River[2] where they will be the first private settlers, but they must wait for their application for a government grant of land to be finalised.[3] It is now late November, and they are becoming anxious.

However, things might have been worse if they hadn't moved out of their expensive Queen Street hotel after that first week back on dry land and taken up residence in the guesthouse farther away from the centre of the town, for, on the night of

December 1st fire breaks out in central Brisbane and the hotel they had first stayed in burns down – as does all the other property in the vicinity of Queen Street. The fire breaks out at about 7.40 pm when a boy knocks a kerosene lamp off a shelf in Stewart and Hemmant's drapery shop on the intersection of Queen and Albert Streets. "Fire!" a lone policeman cries to alert the occupants of the shops, hotels, commercial buildings, and houses in the heart of the little town. Soon the drapery store is burned to the ground and the fire rages onward. Hundreds of people rush to the scene where futile attempts to use tubs of water and the contents of backyard wells do nothing to stop the holocaust which is swiftly engulfing Queen Street.

Jack and Thomasine, hearing the shouting and seeing the flames in the sky, hurry to watch, and Jack, with his army training, soon realises that nobody is in charge and does his best to rally some strong men to try to quell the flames. But without any proper water supply and with only a volunteer fire brigade which has no access to any water (there being no official fire brigade yet) their efforts are thwarted. Chaos increases as furniture of all kinds is hurled out of windows into the street. Chairs, tables, washstands, sofas, pictures, mirrors, are thrown out of windows, and a long high ridge of household items stretches along the middle of the street – a hillock consisting of all sorts of merchandise piled up in the greatest disorder.[4] Before it is finally put out, the fire consumes 50 houses, three hotels, four draperies, two banks – principally the Bank of New South Wales – and many other businesses.

The whole block lying within the boundaries of Queen, George, Elizabeth, and Albert Streets is a mass of smoking ruins and the only places left standing within the block are a building at the corner of Elizabeth and Albert Streets, occupied by Messrs. Ballantyne and M'Nab, coachbuilders. Mason's concert hall, the Real Property Transfer Office and a small cottage adjoining. For two or three days after the fire, Queen Street from Albert Street to George Street is closed. The damage is estimated to be between £60,000 and £100,000,[5] and disrupts normal business in the colony for some while.

****

Early in the New Year of 1865 Jack and Thomasine are finally granted good land on the newly-named Nerang Creek which is soon to be renamed yet again, as the Nerang River, more in keeping with its proportions as a 39-mile- long (62km) main river which rises in the McPherson Range on the Queensland-New South Wales boarder. It then turns north and then east and flows out through the Moreton Bay Broadwater and into the Coral Sea [6]

Thomasine tells her brother William: *"The English Government in order to attract settlers with money in Queensland offered a Thirty Pound land order to first class passengers. We got 1 for me and 1 for my husband and 1 for the children amounting to Ninety Pounds in all."*

Thomasine's mother, Eliza, writing to her son William from Auckland, New Zealand, has less sanguine hopes for Thomasine's future in Australia:

"...I have heard from dear Thomasine. She arrived in Brisbane all right is expecting to increase her family that is a pity I fear she will not like a bush life. I do so pity her poor dear girl. I wish she had come here instead of going there. This is a beautiful country I think you will like it I shall not neglect writing to your sister. I am very anxious about her..." [7]

The next three months are spent in busy preparation for the move. Jack's army experience in setting up camp comes to the fore – they will have to camp on their newly-granted land for some while before they can build a bark hut, let alone a house. As well as purchasing marquees, groundsheets, tents and oil cloths, bedding, oil lamps, candles, matches, axes and basic grocery items and other necessities, Jack orders crop seed, bags of flour, salted meat, cooking implements, mosquito netting, a meat safe, water tanks, a full medical kit, and all the other items vital for the family's survival in the total wilderness, plus a cage of hens and roosters to be supplied to the dock when the expedition is ready to set off south to the Nerang in early April. Jack adds a couple of rifles and a revolver to their baggage. *They might come in handy,* he thinks.

Meanwhile, Thomasine, now six months pregnant, takes her trusty sewing machine out of storage and busies herself making clothes suitable for camping life in the warm, humid climate they are becoming accustomed to.

"May," she tells her daughter, "I'm making very simple dresses for you and me to wear – no petticoats! We will be very busy when we get to the Nerang and we will both have to work hard, so simple cotton dresses are what we'll wear. For Jack and the boys, she runs up work shirts and trousers in tough material, and she also prepares garments for the baby she is expecting.

Each day, she sits down with May and Edward and sets them reading and makes sure they do their sums; *I'm determined the children won't suffer from living in the wilds.*

A few days before the family departs for Nerang, the wife of their guesthouse proprietor approaches Thomasine, and eyeing her obvious state of advanced pregnancy, she ventures to advise her to remain back in Brisbane for the birth rather than risking giving birth in the "complete wilds" without any medical assistance. But Thomasine is adamant:

"Thank you for your kind advice," she replies, "But I'm completely confident my husband will look after me and the baby. After all, it will be my sixth child and I can guide him in what to do – he has had a lot of medical experience in the Army in India. Moreover, there is no way I could travel back from Brisbane to the Nerang with a newborn babe. The Cobb & Co coaches won't be calling in there for some years yet. Because there isn't a proper road[8], the only other way I could travel is on horseback and that would be impossible with a baby, and it would take a week. And anyway, I haven't ridden a horse since I was a child."

Fire!

END NOTES CHAPTER 10

[1] Letter from William, undated, but from its context, 1864.

[2] Following the first official survey of the area by Assistant Surveyor Robert Dixon in May 1840, the Nerang River was initially named the Barrow River, in honour of Sir John Barrow (1764-1848) then the Secretary of the Admiralty. But that name was short-lived, and the name "Nerang" took over. The Queensland Place Names Board notes that the word may have been derived from the Bundjalung language, and refers to either a small river, or shovel-nosed shark.

[3] The first contemporary record of the name Nerang Creek or River being used occurred in 1853, when the Reverend Henry Stobart, tutor to Lord Henry Scott-Montagu and Lord Schomberg Kerr sailed down Moreton Bay By the 1860s, "Nerang" was commonly used in regional newspapers as the name of the waterway that emptied into the Pacific Ocean near the small settlement of Nerang Heads, later renamed Southport. (Ref: http://www.goldcoaststories.com.au/nerang-river/)

[4] *Brisbane's Water Supply: the Queen Street Fire of 1864.* (By Charles Melton.) [Read at a meeting of the Historical Society of Queensland on Sept. 1, 1924.]

[5] After the fire, new buildings, mainly built using stone and brick, were constructed but it was not until 1881 that a Brisbane Fire Brigade Board was established.

[6] In those days, the mouth of the Nerang was at Broadbeach, but the northward drift of sand caused it to spill out by 1930 at Southport.

[7] Letter from Eliza Meredith to her son, William, (no date, but probably late 1864 or early 1865).

[8] It was not until the 1870s that Cobb & Co services began operating to Nerang, via Logan.

11

Nerang

FINALLY, AT THE crack of dawn on that early April morning, it is time to set off. Their camping equipment, food supplies and personal goods and chattels, including several boxes of books they have brought out from England, are loaded on to a dray, and Jack and the children all climb up and journey on it down to the shores of Moreton Bay while Thomasine sits up front next to the driver. Reaching the wharf, they board the cutter Jack has commissioned. He has also hired the services of a strong young labourer to help him pitch the tents and cart the boxes of cargo, including Thomasine's trusty sewing machine, from the cutter to the camp site. The children are now hardened sailors after their long sea voyage, which is fortunate, for the voyage ahead is to prove windy and rough. Toddler Bertie is tied with a rope to prevent him falling overboard, while Edward and May, and Roland, who is now five and old enough to be of help, check the fowls cackling in their cage and find some seed for them. One of their first jobs when they reach the Nerang, Jack tells them, is to help set up the chicken coup. "We can't let them run off into the bushland," he tells the children. "Otherwise we shan't have any eggs for breakfast!"

Jack puts his arm around Thomasine as they stand at the prow of the cutter while the captain and his crew member cast off and they set off along the southern coast of Moreton Bay towards the Coral Sea and the mouth of the Nerang.

"Well, Tommy, time to saddle up! We're on our way at last. Our new life together is really starting!"

Reaching the mouth of the Nerang in 1865 is no easy feat – indeed, it's downright dangerous. The heavily laden cutter has first to carefully negotiate her way along the southern shore of Moreton Bay through a necklace of islands and a barrier of sand and mudbanks amid clusters of mangrove swamps. Some ships, the captain of the cutter tells Jack, have been known to run aground on mudbanks, unable to free their vessels until the spring tide. leaving their passengers and crew marooned for months on end.

The wind is whipping up and the sea becomes very choppy as they turn into the Broadwater with its line of surf to its east, marking the Boat Passage. Finally, they steer into the mouth of the Nerang flowing out into the Coral Sea. The entrance to the river is clogged with sand, and at times the depth of the water is only about five feet (1.5 metres), making navigation a delicate manoeuvre.

They see no-one, not even any of the Aborigines who inhabit the area, which is later to become the Gold Coast and Surfers Paradise. They know of the existence of several European people who inhabit the lower reaches at the mouth of the river – boatmen and timber cutters – but there is no sign of them either. As they negotiate the gravel crossing built to give cedar timber cutters on horseback access to the other side of the river, they anxiously fear they'll run aground. But miraculously, their cutter passes through the eye of the needle and they find themselves out into a broad river, silent except for birdcalls and the rhythmic chirping of crickets, and shrouded in luxuriant foliage: towering cedars, eucalypts and tropical palms dripping with vines which reach down to the water's edge. From time-to-time, a large fish plops up through the water, leaving a circle of ripples behind it.

Nerang River greatly-tamed vegetation today

They pass by the big cotton plantations on either side of the river which have been established by the Manchester

Queensland Cotton Company Limited, run by Edmund Henry Price from the Lancashire milling town of Bury, who had bought a £1000 share in the Manchester Company and has been appointed its general manager. He's the self-declared "King Cotton" of Nerang, and a man of grandiloquent habits and tastes.

Jack has heard about Price's exploits, which are the talk of Brisbane pubs, and he tells Thomasine what he knows about Price's profligate activities, which, coupled with the recent disastrous floods of March 1864, are creating ever-larger debts as Price mortgages parts of the estate while continuing on his merry ways. He installs his manager, Robert Muir, on part of his land to set up a sugar plantation, (*Benowa*) and later, a mill,

"Already the estate on our right," says Jack, pointing to an empty-looking expanse of partly cultivated land, "is almost completely closed down. But his *Bundall* estate on the left is still going well. Edmund Henry Price has a house on *Bundall* with stables and accommodation for his overseer and some German workers, and he holds extravagant parties there where visitors can drink all they can hold – and more. But the talk of Brisbane is that it can't last much longer, although he's still the "darling" of Brisbane society and is a welcome guest at Government House."[1]

After they pass by the Manchester cotton estates, their cutter sails for several miles up-river through silent waters with no sign of human occupation on either side – apart from the very occasional, fleeting, vision of a dusky figure flitting between the trees.

"Aborigines," says Jack, "I believe there are hundreds of them in the Nerang area. I believe they belong to the Yugambeh tribe and they've lived here for thousands of years. Some of them find work on the cotton estates and I hear they work well when they feel like it."

Thomasine gives an involuntary shiver at the sight of the Aborigines. *I hope we don't suffer the same fate as my poor Father and brother did,* she silently prays.

Finally, their cutter reaches the stretch of water leading towards the end of the navigable part of the Nerang, and Jack and the captain consult the survey map they have brought to identify exactly where the Browne allotment is located. They drop anchor as close as possible to the right-hand bank of the river and in a frenzy of activity begin unloading the vessel. The captain and Jack carefully help the now eight-months pregnant Thomasine and two-year-old Bertie down to the riverbank and then the other children and the fowls in their cage are unloaded.

Feeling the sand under her feet as she steps off the cutter, Thomasine is overwhelmed by a sense of achievement – and relief. The cosy comfort of her London life seems a long way in the past as she sets foot on their new piece of Southern Hemisphere property. Jack, relying on his army experience, then starts clearing a section of low scrub not far from the river, where he lays down the groundsheets and then, with the help of his hired labourer, they erect the tents – one for the children and one for Jack and Thomasine, linked by a covered canopy of groundsheets. He has sensibly brought finely-netted fabric to hang over the beds to ward off mosquitoes and the myriad other insect predators they have already observed on their way up the river. The nets will also act as a wall of defence against the inroads of snakes and spiders, some of which are deadly.

Thomasine and May unpack the culinary basics and find a packing case to use as a table and use smaller boxes for chairs on the area outside the tents. It's time for lunch and the family hungrily devours the food their guesthouse has provided for the first day and night under canvas.

After lunch, Jack and the labourer dig holes for two latrines "One for the ladies and the other for the gents," as Jack explains, "far enough away from our sleeping and eating quarters."

"What happens when the holes get full up?" asks Edward, who has an inquiring mind.

"Then we fill the holes in with earth and dig new holes elsewhere," Jack explains. "Eventually the old holes mix into the earth all around them. A more fancy version with walls and a door is called an 'earth closet'. We'll have some of them later."

Next Jack and the boys stake out a poultry run and build a chicken coup from some nearby saplings and bark to ensure no hens or roosters escape.

"We must make sure we keep the roosters separate from most of the hens," Jack explains to Edward and Roland,

"Otherwise, we'll have too many baby chickens and no free eggs to eat."

Meanwhile, Thomasine has rigged up a clothesline, ready for her first clothes wash. "I'm a real tiger about washing," she tells May. "I inherited it from my mother, and also from my grandmother, when I stayed with her and grandpa at Stoke Prior. You've probably inherited it too., I think it runs in our family."

Jack starts carrying buckets of water from the river and boils the water over a fire he lights before pouring the clean water for drinking into one of the tanks he has brought.

"I hope it will rain soon, to help fill these tanks. I know this isn't the rainy season, but we should get a drop or two," he says. "And we need to search around for a little spring or stream. I must say, though, that the river water looks pretty clean too."

By now, Thomasine is feeling decidedly weary. *It has all been so extraordinary,* she muses, *in fact, ever since we left England I've been in a kind of dream. But here we are at last, at our new home, and it's a beautiful, strange, place, like nothing I have ever seen before, completely different from the gentle English countryside of Stoke Prior, or the dark Yorkshire hills, or Paris – and so totally unlike London! I think I'm going to like it a lot. And now I must busy myself getting the children's mattresses ready in their tent and making somewhere comfortable for Jack and myself in our tent. It's certainly going to be an adventure. I also need to get out the oil lamps and prepare to light one later for the children, so they don't wake up in the night, frightened.*

By late afternoon, the cutter has been emptied and the captain bids farewell as he sets off back down river with his crew member and the labourer, in time to catch the tide back into Moreton Bay.

That evening the family sits on empty packing cases around the fire and devours the rest of the guesthouse food. "I think we should call this place *Keith Farm*," Jack suggests, "after Uncle Keith."

"Tomorrow," says Thomasine, "May and I will make some bread from the flour we've brought, and we'll roast some of the meat I got from the butcher in Brisbane. I've hung it in the meat safe to keep the flies away but it won't last long in this heat.

Those hens had better start laying soon or we'll go hungry! And we'll get some fishing lines out tomorrow and start catching some of those fish we saw jumping in the river as we sailed up."

"Are there cwocodiles?" asks Roland.

"Yes," replied Jack, "and sharks – bull sharks.[2] I'll make a swimming area for you soon, safe from crocodiles and sharks. But first we need to get the place ready for sowing maize and then cotton. So I'll be very busy for a while and I'll need you boys to help me."

They wash their dishes in some of the extra, unboiled, water Jack has brought from the river, noting how pure it looks, and after Thomasine says prayers with the children, they all fall into a deep sleep. It has been a very busy day.

Jack and Thomasine sit outside their tent for a while, soaking up the darkness and the total solitude of their new abode.

"Look at the stars," Jack exclaims. "I can see the Great South Star, and other stars. They look so clear in this air." Thomasine soaks in the enormous solitude of their new home, as she wrote later to her brother William:

"We settled at Nerang Creek April 1865 and the family were the first settlers in the district. There were blacks in hundreds and no white people for a few miles." [3]

They then retire for their first night's sleep on *Keith Farm*, but around 10 pm, they are awakened by a loud sound, a weird moaning, throbbing sound coming from the bush not far away. Then they hear loud cries and singing and a high-pitched whistling sound, followed by endless moaning and throbbing from some kind of instrument.

"That sound is dark yellow-brown," says Thomasine, sitting up suddenly in bed. "It sounds like some kind of wind instrument, as if it's coming from a wooden trumpet or something."

"I think it must be the Aborigines," Jack says. "But what do you mean by 'it sounds yellow-brown'?" he asks, puzzled. "Well," Thomasine replies. "Don't all sounds have a colour? That musical instrument sounds yellow-brown to me."

Jack is more puzzled. "No, I don't see colours when I hear sounds," he says. "Tell me more."

"Well," Thomasine continues. "For me, every sound – a note on a piano, an orchestra, birds singing or twittering, people's voices, letters of the alphabet, numbers – they all have colours. I couldn't imagine what it would be like not to have music in colours – or anything else. It enriches my world."[4]

"Tommy, you never cease to surprise me," Jack says, giving her a hug. But he is secretly concerned by the loud noise which continues to come from the Aborigines in the clearing. *I surely hope we haven't wandered into big trouble,* he thinks, with a shiver.

And so ends their first day – a momentous day – and the Browne family will become celebrated as "the pioneer family of the Nerang".

END NOTES CHAPTER 11

[1] Longhurst, Robert *NERANG SHIRE A HISTORY to 1949 [Nerang.]* Price and his cotton empire are soon to suffer a sorry end. After his funds run out, cotton farming is superseded by sugar and other crops and the properties are finally sold. By the 1880s Price has become a shambling figure in a ragged overcoat and broken-down shoes with no socks, wandering the back streets of Brisbane cadging money from passers-by to purchase drink. By 1896, at the age of 60, he is admitted to the Dulwich Benevolent Asylum, but later released until 1903 when he is readmitted and dies from gout and heart disease.

[2] A few crocodiles still exist in the Nerang River

[3] Letter quoted in *Two Families, op cit.*

[4] This phenomenon is Synaesthesia. I cannot prove that Thomasine was a Synaesthete, but Synaesthesia is more likely to be passed down through the female line in families. It also occurs in several of Thomasine's descendants, including this author, and cousin Genevieve Grainger.

12

A Pair of Timber Cutters

NEXT MORNING, after a somewhat fretful sleep, disturbed by the endless noise of singing, chanting and weird-sounding musical instruments coming from the bush they're awakened at dawn by their roosters' crowing, and from time-to-time by the sound of loud cackling laughter which they eventually track down to a brown-feathered bird which perches in a gum tree near their tent. "That must be a laughing jackass," Jack decides. (He is yet to know it by its Australian name: "kookaburra".)

After two days of heavy labour, cutting down trees and clearing scrub, Jack realises he needs more help, otherwise he won't get his first crop of cotton planted by winter.

"I'm going to need some labourers," he tells Thomasine, "So I'm going to have to walk downstream to the cotton plantation – it'll take me a while as it's over 16 miles. There should be one or two of those Germans workers there who'll soon be out of a job now that one of the plantations is on its last legs. And I'll also see if I might be able to buy a horse from the manager."

"But how will you get down to the cotton plantations? Thomasine asks. "There's no road?".

"I noticed a track along the banks of the river much of the way – no doubt used by the Aborigines, and probably the timber cutters," Jack says, referring to the practice of the timber cutters floating their valuable cedar logs downstream to be loaded on to cutters and shipped to Sydney or Brisbane, where the glowing dark reddish wood is fashioned into polished floorboards and drawing-room doors and dining tables for the mansions of Sydney's Darling Point and Bellevue Hill and for the terrace houses in the better parts of Glebe, or perhaps for the new buildings going up in Queen Street Brisbane to replace the ones gutted in the 1864 fire.

But it turns out Jack doesn't have to walk for over 16 miles down-river to find some assistants, for, three days after the family arrives, two muscular timber cutters carrying swags on their backs emerge from the river bank on horseback, tie up their horses to a tree and introduce themselves to Jack and Thomasine as Edmund Harper and William Duncan.

****

Jack doesn't yet realise quite how fortuitous is the arrival of Edmund Harper and William Duncan; they will provide him with far more than just manual labour in tree-felling and land clearing, for they are both, and particularly Edmund, old hands on the Northern Rivers of NSW and now the Nerang area. They will provide Jack with invaluable advice and information about what is happening round-and-about, and will give him useful tips on farming in this semi-tropical, flood-prone country.

Edmund is already a local legend, having arrived at the Tweed River possibly as early as 1842. He was born in Nottingham in 1826 and arrived in Sydney in 1831 at the age of five with his parents Gilbert and Maria. His father, Gilbert, a fitter and turner, had been transported to NSW as a convict for a crime (unknown) he had committed, but was granted a ticket-of-leave in 1843 as a free man. However, he transgressed again a year later for "defacing" currency and was transported to Norfolk Island. His wife, Maria, described by the locals as a "virago" lived in a hut and warned off any intruders with a shotgun. By this time, their son Edmund had learned the timber cutting trade and had arrived on the Tweed to join the handful of rough, rowdy cedar cutters encamped by the river, many of them escaping the law for one reason or another.

He had later returned for a time to Sydney where he worked with two brothers of the Milson family, whom he helped with droving tasks, bringing their herds from Wallumbine on the far North Coast of NSW down to what he called "their place on the North Shore" (later named Milsons Point).

In those very early days there were only 25 or so timber cutters in the NSW Northern Rivers area, but by the 1830s many more had come, some bringing wives, and setting up permanent abodes. Some of these men, armed with guns, clashed badly with the local Aborigines, who, up till that time, had mainly got along well with any Europeans they encountered, guiding them through the dense bush and trading with them for flour, tobacco, and other items. The problem grew after the European newcomers' activities began to threaten the natives' traditional food supplies of bandicoots, possums and wallabies as well as their fishing grounds which provided snapper, flathead and bream, and, closer to the shore, pipis and other shellfish. The introduction of Native Police exacerbated the trouble because Aborigines were now pitted against not only Europeans, but some other Aborigines. The State of Queensland had the largest population of Aborigines in Australia, but their numbers were fast depleting, due mainly to "white men's diseases" such as smallpox (there was a major outbreak in 1831, killing at least 30 Aborigines), the common cold, and measles. Moreover, as time went on, many incidents and some major atrocities were to occur as timber cutters and pastoralists moved north, further decimating the native population.[1]

Edmund ("Neddy") Harper, following the cedar trail, gradually moves north to the Barrow (Nerang) area where he usually cuts down the trees with the help of a partner. But he is by nature a loner and is regarded by the timber-cutting community as an eccentric old timer who lives much of his days in a close relationship with the local Kombumerri clan, part of the Yugambeh tribe, taking an Aboriginal girl as his "wife", and learning their language. (He even talks in his sleep in an Aboriginal dialect).

This, then, is the man, who, with his timber-cutting partner, William Duncan, has offered his services to Jack that late April day in 1865. Edmund and William make a deal to Jack: in return for a good share of the proceeds from the sale of the cedar they'll fell on the Browne allotment, they will help clear the land ready for farming. Jack accepts their offer instantly and the two men pitch their tent farther down towards the riverbank, and, taking their axes from their swags, get down to work immediately. By nightfall a small section of land has been cleared of trees and Jack sighs with relief. The two men go back to their tent and soon the odour of sizzling wallaby steak wafts up from their fire.

After dinner, Thomasine gets the children ready for bed and Jack invites the two men up to his campfire for a yarn about the Nerang area over a beer

"Come and join us, Tommy!" Jack calls out, and Thomasine comes and sits down with them for a while, enjoying the stories Edmund and William are relating about characters they've come across down on the Logan and Tweed Rivers, where quite a few Europeans are now settled. Then Thomasine gets up and bids goodnight "I'm pretty weary," she explains, "We haven't been getting much sleep the last few days with the noise the Aborigines make in the bush."

"Yes," says Duncan "You've gone and planted yourselves right near a traditional Abo Bora and Kipper Ring.[2]

Thomasine pricks up her ears at this and settles back on her packing-case seat.

"What in God's name is a Bora and Kipper Ring?" asks Jack, bewildered.

"A Bora isn't the same as a corroboree," Edmund explains, "it's a special, religious kind of ceremony – it's both the name for the ceremony and for the special ground it's held on. And a Kipper is a young male who is initiated into the tribe. They're words that have filtered up from down around the Hunter region, and the local Abos here probably have their own words for them. But a Bora is made up of two circles marked in the ground with a hollowed out pathway running in between them. The outer circle is a public tribal area and the inner circle is a secret, private, area where the young 14 or 15.year old Aborigine male is initiated into the tribe. Before that, he has a name given to him by his mother, and he lives with the females of the tribe. But once he steps into the Bora Ring like the one next to us here – and they go through the ceremony, they are given a new name and become a Kipper, which means they become a member of the tribe and are allowed to carry a spear and fight."

Thomasine and Jack are fascinated by what they are hearing.

"Tell us more, Edmund," urges Thomasine.

"Very few whites have ever witnessed a Bora," Edmund goes on. "But I've been privileged to see some because I'm more or less part of the tribe now. The lay-out of a Bora site mirrors the Milky Way. They invite other members of their clan – the males – to witness the Bora, then when it's over they go in for a mock battle, though often someone does get killed. Then they all go off together and hunt and come back and have a feast."

"It all seems to go on for a very long time," says Jack, referring to the nightly performances in the clearing next to their camp.

"Yes, it *is* going on for a particularly long time," Edmund agrees. "I suspect it's because they want to warn you that this is their territory. They're making a big song and dance about it. They don't regard themselves as owners of the territory, the land, but they believe they're part of it. They're spiritually connected to it."

Thomasine, her head reeling with this information, tells Edmund about how the Maoris murdered her father and brother.

"Could the Aborigines do that to us?" she asks.

"No, it's very unlikely they'd cause you any harm," Edmund replies. "The Abos are very different from the Maori – a completely different race. They do fight a lot, like the Maori, but mainly it's inter-tribal or clan fighting – and they don't go in for modern weapons like the Maori. The Abos tend to use boomerangs and stones, and for close-up combat they use their spears and shields. The Abos don't cultivate the land – like the Maori – either. They just live off it. I don't think you have any need for worry, Mrs Browne. They're simply demonstrating that this is their sacred ground."

Relieved to hear this, Thomasine bids the men goodnight and falls into bed thankfully, not caring that "bed" is now just a thin mattress laid straight onto the groundsheet in their tent.

Jack stays on with Edmund and William and learns some more about the ceremony.

"I didn't want to mention in front of a lady what else goes on at a Bora," Edmund says, "But they do all kinds of things to the young men who are being initiated into the customs of the tribe. They often circumcise them. Some tribes pull out a tooth from the boy. Then they make patterned cuts all over their chests and backs and fill the cuts with dried grass and sand. The initiated young men then have to wait in total silence for days on end till their wounds have healed, leaving marks on the skin, and then they join the men, and the first thing they do is hold a mock fight with each other to prove they are able to handle a spear."

Jack sits silently for a while and sips his beer. "Edmund, you've given me a lot of food for thought," he says.

"By the way," Edmund adds, as he, too, gets up to leave the campfire. "I notice your missus is pretty far gone. When's baby due?" he asks.

"Any day now," Jack replies.

"If you need any help, the Abo women are very good midwives," Edmund says. "Let me know if you'd like their help."

Jack thanks him but says he thinks he can cope. "I had a bit of that kind of experience in the Army camps in India," he says. "Quite a few wives and other women tagged along with the troops."

****

A week or so later, Jack decides he must have a horse. *I'll need to somehow get to Brisbane once Tommy has the baby – or we'll run out of supplies,* he decides – and anyway, Jack without a horse is not the true Jack. He borrows one of the timber cutters' horses and follows their instructions on how to find the bush trails leading to the mouth of the Nerang. He returns next morning, still riding the timber cutter's horse and leading a sturdy-looking mare and her foal.

"The mare looks like being a good stayer. I can't call her Dobbin, as she's a mare, but Polly sounds a reliable kind of name," he tells Thomasine, "she's no thoroughbred, but she'll get me to Brisbane and back no matter how tough the going gets. And I'll break in the foal for the boys to learn to ride. I'll get you up on Polly, too, Tommy, once you've had the babe. I know you used to enjoy riding with your father all those years ago at Tring."

Thomasine is beginning to relax and enjoy her new environment, as she says in her letter to her brother William: *"We are come to live in this world and like it very well."* The children are starting to look healthier than

88

they've ever been, with their skin tanning brown in the sun. They have taken up fishing with alacrity and have already supplied enough catches to fill the lunch and dinner tables twice. The hens have started to lay, and Thomasine is planting vegetable seeds in a patch not far from their cooking area which Jack has prepared for her kitchen garden. The milling flies and other insects are a perennial nuisance, but Thomasine manages to shield the food as best she can with muslin netting.

"I'm very happy here," Thomasine tells Jack, "but I do miss my piano."

"We'll make sure you have one soon," Jack promises.

"What? In a tent?" Thomasine asks.

"We won't be living in a tent forever," Jack assures her. "I plan to build a house before too long."

Only one worry intrudes into this bucolic scene: the endless night-time activities of the Aborigines in their Kipper Ring, and the stealthy nocturnal intrusion into their camp site by young Aboriginal boys who silently creep around the tents, stealing on one occasion, a pair of Thomasine's earrings, and on another night, a set of silver spoons she has brought out from England.

Jack, too, is concerned at these nocturnal intrusions. He fears that the new baby, when it arrives, might fascinate the natives.

"We'll build a fence around our land," he finally declares. "I suspect that some of that hullaballoo they're creating night-in, night-out is to demonstrate to us that we are intruding into their domain. We need to stand up for our rights too."

With the help of Edmund and William, Jack builds a sturdy post and pole fence and covers it with brushwood and bark, and he places a gate in the fence opposite their tents. The nightly clamour from the Bora and Kipper Ring continues, and Thomasine listens to the throbbing sound of the didgeridoos and starts to understand the music.

"I'm beginning to hear the rhythms in their music," she tells Jack. "It's very different from the European music I'm used to, but I'm slowly understanding it and I'm finding it very complex. But I must say it would be lovely to have a silent evening so we could all get some proper sleep."

Each evening now, before Thomasine says prayers with the children, Jack sits down with them in their tent and starts reading from *Swiss Family Robinson*. The children are entranced with this tale of a family of German children and their parents marooned on an island after their ship is wrecked *en route* to Port Jackson in Australia.

"It's just like us!" Edward exclaims.

"Yes." Jack agrees, "But at least they had more animals. We need a cow next, so we can have some fresh milk. This powdered stuff in your cocoa doesn't taste too good.

"Now it's your turn, May, to read some of the book, and then Edward can have a go. And soon, Roland, you'll be able to read too, if you listen to your mother's lessons."

Gradually the children drift off to sleep and Jack goes back to the campfire to join Thomasine to sit under the stars until it's time for bed.

Each night Thomasine goes back into their tent to check the children are safe. On several occasions she has spotted a fleeting dark figure running away from the tent, and on one occasion she confronts a young Aboriginal boy who looks at her with startled eyes and runs off. *These boys hardly ever steal anything. They seem to be just curious about us,* Thomasine decides. *But we need to stop them somehow from coming.*

END NOTES CHAPTER 12

[1] It is impossible to know exactly how many Aborigines died from conflicts with Europeans in Queensland, but some experts claim the number to be at least 250,000.

[2] (i) *Queensland Times*, September 2nd 1948

(ii) *Australian Archaeology*, No. 77, Preprint. Astronomical Orientations of Bora Ceremonial Grounds in Southeast Australia. Robert S. Fuller1,2 , Duane W. Hamacher1,3 and Ray P. Norris1,2,4 1 Warawara – Department of Indigenous Studies, Macquarie University, NSW,.

13

Born in a Tent

IT IS NOW LATE APRIL and winter is on the way – or what there is of a winter in that balmy semi-tropical region. The rainfall is likely to taper off, but Jack has found a natural spring tucked away in the far reaches of the allotment, supplying them with plenty of cool fresh water. Thomasine also finds the spring water ideal for keeping food cool by storing it in the creek bed.

Edmund and William are continuing with their tree lopping and Jack has planted a crop of maize.

On the evening of May 8th, Thomasine tells Jack she thinks the baby is due.

"I know the symptoms, from already having had five children," she tells Jack. "It's due any moment now."

After dinner, with the children tucked up in their beds, Jack hastily prepares for the birth. He takes his medical bag out and checks it and re-lights the fire to boil up the requisite saucepans of hot water.

"I'm not really sure what all this hot water is supposed to be for," he says.

"Nor do I," says Thomasine, laughing. "It's just that everyone always does it."

Jack places clean towels straight off the clothesline, ready for the big moment, and Thomasine lies down on the bed, her stomach contracting every now and then.

"The baby's on the way," she says, and Jack holds her hand. Thomasine gives him instructions on exactly what to do and how to cut the cord – as she has said, she's highly experienced in childbirth.

"I'm likely to make a bit of noise towards the end," she warns Jack. "I hope I don't wake the children."

"Don't worry, Tommy, the Bora and Kipper activities will be in full swing soon – the children won't hear a thing. And Edmund and Duncan's tent is quite a long way down the field."

As midnight approaches, Thomasine's contractions quicken and, no matter how hard she tries to stifle them, her groans of pain begin. As the pain increases, Jack takes out a small bottle of liquid from his medicine chest and sprinkles it on a handkerchief and holds it to Thomasine's nose.

"This will help a little, my darling, it's chloroform," Jack says, "Queen Victoria used it when she was giving birth a few years ago. We often used it in the Army to reduce pain."

The chloroform helps and Thomasine is able to relax a little. Shortly after midnight on May 9th, she gives birth to a baby girl. Jack is calm and competent, tying and cutting the cord as instructed (and as he has done in the past in India on the women who follow the soldiers), and dealing with the other contingencies of childbirth. Then he wraps the baby in a shawl and hands her to Thomasine.

"I'm so proud of you, Tommy. She's beautiful – and I love her little tuft of red hair" he says.

As Thomasine later reports in a letter to William[1]:

> "I was confined of a little girl (and now we have 5 children between us) she is a fine child and Jack is so proud of her. We are going to call her Thomasine. Just fancy being tied up in a tent, no doctor, nurse or attendant. Jack had to be all in one and how good he was to me."

The new baby's name, "Thomasine", is soon converted to "Thomasina", to avoid confusion with her mother's name, and swiftly shortened by everyone to "Ina" – to further avoid confusion. But she is soon to get yet another name too, for, a week after the baby is born, Thomasine hatches her big plan:

"Jack, I think we need to make a gesture to the Aborigines. Obviously, they feel we are trespassing on their territory – land they have used for their ceremonies for thousands of years. They don't understand British Land Law. So we need to offer them something as a gesture.

"What I suggest is that you put on your best Army uniform to look important and take a bag of flour to the Kipper Ring, while I bring the baby to show them. May can carry a cake she has baked, and the boys can simply come along and play the bugle. We'll stand to attention and Edward can sound your old bugle – that should alert them.".

"Do you mean we're going to offer Ina as a human sacrifice?" asked Jack, only half joking.

"Of course not!" Thomasine retorts. "Over my dead body! But I have heard that Aborigines in other districts cherish white babies, because they've never seen them before."

And so, a day or two later Jack, Thomasine, holding the baby, and May and the boys stand near the Kipper Ring while Edward blows the bugle.

The Aboriginal tribesmen and their women emerge from the bush, holding back at first. Then they spot Thomasine holding out the baby towards them. Stepping forward, the leader of the tribe comes up close to the baby and points at her, declaring: "Bingarabah Erran" (Bingarabah being the name of the "place where she comes from" and Erran, "girl".) Thomasine then holds up the baby for all the tribe to see, and they clap their hands together and cheer at the pretty little pale-skinned baby with her fluff of red hair. Jack offers the tribal leader the bag of flour, and May holds out the cake to the head woman of the tribe.

From that moment on, the Aborigines and the Brownes co-exist quite happily. The Aborigines are soon trading seafood, bush fruits and nuts for flour and tobacco. As baby Ina first crawls, and later toddles into the bushland, the Aborigines pick her up and bring her back to the safety of the camp, and gradually some of them start working with Jack in the fields, and a few of the women help Thomasine with her cooking activities. In return for their help, Jack gives them bags of flour which they find useful, not just for making damper, but also for mending wounded warriors' cuts, and bruises to their heads. As time goes on, Jack will pay the Aborigines money which they can use as the Nerang area develops and shops open.

The activities in the Bora continue sporadically, but they are never as noisy now. Indeed, the last corroboree and inter-tribal fight of the Yugambeh people will be held near Burleigh in 1871. Also, in 1871, in August, the Queensland Government, perhaps guilty over the decline of the Aborigines in southern Queensland, grants the Aborigines about 100 acres of land running four miles from north to south in the Nerang Valley on the western side of the river. The Lutheran Mission,[2] which had earlier established a mission on the Albert River, had first applied for the land in 1869 to establish an "Aboriginal Industrial Mission Reserve," to be run by Hausemann and two other missionaries. It was finally established in 1871, and about 100 Aborigines worked quite peacefully, tilling a portion of the land, until other tribesmen arrived and fighting broke out. As time wears on, however, the Aborigines show little aptitude for either organised work or conversion to the Lutheran faith and the experiment peters out. On January 25th 1879 the Mission Reserve on the Nerang River is officially cancelled by notice in the *Government Gazette* and, under pressure from new settlers, keen to take up this particularly fertile land, the vacated land is quickly put up for sale.

****

Meanwhile, back to 1865. Jack, helped by Edmund, William and young Edward and Roland, perseveres with his maize and cotton crops. Work starts every morning around 6 am and Jack and his young stepsons and their handful of Aboriginal helpers find it an uphill battle to clear away the ever-encroaching weeds that flourish in that swampy soil. The maize is sprouting well but the cotton is proving a problem. Although cotton has been grown around Moreton Bay since convict days nobody seems to know how to grow it properly in the swampy, semi-tropical conditions of the Nerang. Even by the time Jack is trying to grow his first crop nobody knows for sure whether it should be replanted every year or left for a year to harvest a second crop from it, nor how thickly it should be planted. Jack, having picked up knowledge from the Brisbane pubs, decides to plant the Sea Island or Upland variety, but he isn't sure that it's the right choice. It proves to be a difficult crop to tend with no pesticides to fight the caterpillars that eat the crops, and noxious weeds perpetually encroaching. Jack, being a small farmer, can expect to harvest only a few bales and certainly won't be able to make a living from it, despite receiving a government subsidy.

"I think we'll move on to growing sugar cane next season," Jack tells Thomasine. This is a wise decision. With the American Civil War ending in 1865 cotton farming resumes in the south of America and cotton prices will gradually return to pre-war levels and the English cotton mills are soon back to normal production.

END NOTES CHAPTER 13

[1] Thomasine's letter to William (no date).

Regina Ganter, Griffith University "German Missionaries in Australia" A web-directory of international encounters.

[2] Lena Cooper's unpublished Manuscript pp308-9.(Local Studies Library in Southport.), quoted in Two *Families, ibid.*

14

A Trip to Brisbane

"IT'S TIME I went up to Brisbane," Jack declares one morning, a month or so after Ina's birth. "We need some salted meat until we can get our hands on some farm animals, and I need to order more farm equipment. I'll see if I can share one of the cotton peoples' regular cutters to bring back what I order. Let me know what you need for the household, Tommy. And write some letters to the family for me to take to send off. I'll pick up our mail, and some newspapers too. Heaven knows what's been going on in the big wide world while we've been here in our little patch of paradise!"

Jack has wisely given a Brisbane address for all mail coming to them – the postman only very occasionally calls in at Nerang on his weekly trip from Brisbane down to the settlements on the Logan and Tweed. After all, nobody, or virtually nobody, is yet living on the Nerang. And where would a postman deliver any letters to? The best – the only – place is the big cotton estate.

Jack is going to find his trip to Brisbane and back arduous. The rough tracks made by the very early cattle teams from William Duckett White's properties on the Tweed in the 1850s, and a little later, timber cutters' trails that linked the fledgling communities of the Nerang, Mudgeeraba and the Tallebudgera (called by the locals the 'Tallebuggera' until the name is made more "polite" in 1875) were only navigable by horseback. Carts and buggies couldn't cope with the mud and steep inclines. It won't be until 1870 that anything like a road linking the Nerang to Brisbane will be considered.

Jack prepares carefully for his trip, binding his reliable mare Polly's legs with canvas to protect them from the razor-sharp "lawyer vine" that grows all over the riverbank – "Once you get tangled with lawyers you never get out" is what the locals say. He has checked with Edmund where to locate Aboriginal tracks and timber cutters' trails. He packs some salted meat and flour for damper, and some matches to make a fire, and takes a bottle with him to re-fill with water from the plentiful streams. Wrapping everything, including his rifle and an axe, into a blanket, he saddles up Polly, hugs the children and kisses Thomasine goodbye and sets off on his trek to Brisbane which will take up to a week, depending on the weather and his make-shift map.

While Jack is away, Thomasine busies herself with her vegetable garden, planting more seeds and potatoes and digging further beds for more plants. She has recovered quickly from the birth of Ina and is back to her usual energetic self. The boys, still revelling in the freedom of their new outdoor life, catch fish – perch and bream – and help with the gardening while May looks after baby Ina and toddler Bertie. The washing flutters on the clothesline each morning and Thomasine declares herself content. *My life in freezing old England seems such a long way away,* she thinks. *Having to sort out the menu every day with Cook and wrapping up the children in winter clothes. And all that bronchitis! – no longer! All I miss is my piano, but I'll just have to wait for one for the moment.* Occasionally, dark memories of the death of young Amelia, and her first husband, Edward James, and the murder of her father and brother flash through her mind, but she banishes them. *Life in this new country is sunny and happy. I have a good husband and a fine family. What more can I want?*

Thomasine in casual dress

She is glad, however, to have Edmund Harper and William Duncan still camping down near the river – they make her feel safe. They come and go now, having found a new stand of cedar about half-a-mile away, which they fell and bring back to the big sandbank and tie the logs up to start their journey down-river. Some of the local Aborigines come to see her, offering her firewood, crabs and shellfish and help her carry water from the spring, and she repays their help with flour and biscuits. She hopes Jack will order plenty more flour when he's in Brisbane – otherwise, they'll starve.

Twenty three days later, Jack, looking heavily bearded, and tanned from the sun, his clothes coated with dry mud, rides back to the camp, dismounts and ties Polly to a tree, giving her a good rub down after the long trek.

Then he runs up to Thomasine and embraces her. "Tommy, my darling! How I have missed you! And where are the children?" Jack exclaims.

"They'll be back by dinnertime," Thomasine says, "Their stomachs are better than alarm clocks."

She wryly observes Jack's brown face and muddied clothes, *To think he used to wear lavender kid gloves!*

A heavily bearded Jack

They walk back to the tent and Jack goes inside to take a peep at the sleeping Ina.

"All's well," he says. "You've done a good job in my absence, Tommy."

"Now, Jack," Thomasine says, "Tell me all about Brisbane. Who did you see? What news have you? Did you pick up any letters?"

They sit down outside their tent and Jack opens a large sack he has brought back with him. "I found it tough going in some parts of the bush, where there's no road at all," he tells Thomasine. "Fortunately, I had my axe and I was able to hack through the undergrowth to make a path for Polly and me to follow. But we finally found a road not far from Brisbane and we got along faster after that.

"Brisbane looks quite a lot different already," he goes on. "It's amazing how much building work is happening there so soon after that big fire in the centre of the town – they're starting to replace all the old wooden buildings that got burnt down.

"The new town will be more of a city when all the work is finished. Many of the old wooden buildings are being replaced with stone and they'll be a lot grander than the old structures.

"I picked up our mail and the newspapers – and I placed orders for a number of items we need for the farm – and what you need for our camp," he adds. "Everything will come down here to Nerang Heads in the next coastal ship from Brisbane. What we need now is our own boat so we can pick up everything and sail it back up the river. I'll start looking for a boat to buy tomorrow."

Thomasine picks up a letter from her mother, Eliza. "As usual, she's trying to persuade me to settle in New Zealand, not Australia. Too late, I'm afraid. And here's a letter from my dear sister, Mary. I haven't heard from her for a long while. She must be 21 by now, and already married with two young children! How time flies! I think I might do a reverse of my mother's advice and see if I can persuade Mary to bring her family over here to settle."

Jack shows Thomasine a letter from his mother: "Listen to this, Tommy. Mother says Uncle Keith and her younger sister, Louisa, are now a "couple" and plan to become engaged shortly!

Poor Louisa has had a dreadful time. Her husband treated her abysmally, beating her quite often. They divorced at one time but then, silly woman, she re-joined him. But the marriage is finally over, and Uncle Keith has stepped in to provide for her. As you once said, Tommy, Uncle Keith is a champion of damsels in distress!"

Thomasine smiles "Louisa will become Lady Ball eventually, when they marry," she says. "Well, I wish her good luck. She deserves some happiness. Your ties to Uncle Keith grow ever tighter!"

"How old is Uncle Keith now?" Jack asks. "He must be well into his late seventies by now."

Thomasine begins scanning the Brisbane papers and starts to laugh. "There's a lovely item here about the scandal at the Queensland Post Office in Brisbane over missing sums of money in the Money-Order Branch," she says, reading out a report in the *Rockhampton Bulletin and Central Queensland Advertiser:*

> "Between Mrs. Barney, the head of this branch, (a lady who is without doubt an ornament to society in private life, but whose sex and qualifications do not fit her to be the head of a Government office,) and Mr. Prior, her superior in the official acceptation of the term, there has been a long-standing feud, which feud has been in a great measure the cause of all the irregularities which have lately come to light."

"Poor Mrs Barney!" Thomasine exclaims. "I suspect it was she who discovered the corrupt activities in the department and now she's taking the blame!"

Jack is perusing the London newspapers – *The Times, Telegraph,* and *Illustrated London News*, dating back a couple of months because of their long trip by ship to Brisbane.

"Now here's some big news, Tommy. The American Civil War is finally at an end. The Confederates are routed, and Abraham Lincoln has won the day!"

"That is big news!" Thomasine says. "Tell me more."

Jack leafs through the pile of papers. "Here's another big item!" he says pointing to a page reporting that General Robert E. Lee had surrendered the Confederation Army to general Ulysses S. Grant at Appomattox Court House in Virginia on April 9th, 1865,

"That's important news indeed," Jack remarks, turning to the next paper in the pile he has brought from Brisbane.

"But this is even bigger, shocking news!" he exclaims. "On April 14th the Stars and Stripes was ceremoniously raised over Fort Lauderdale, and the triumphant President Lincoln celebrated by going to the theatre that night with his wife, Mary, where they were to see the play "Our American Cousin" but during the third Act, a man called John Wilkes Booth shot the president in the head!" Jack pauses. "This is terrible news!"

He goes on reading. "Apparently doctors attended the President, but he never recovered consciousness and died the following morning. My God…"

The last paper Jack has brought back from Brisbane records that the following month the remaining Confederate forces surrender, thus ending America's Civil War.

Both Jack and Thomasine are silent for a moment. Then Jack says thoughtfully. "That is world news, but for us, here on the Nerang River, the end to the American Civil War means we must give up thinking of growing cotton – the southern American states will start up their cotton production and exportation again and England won't need cotton any longer from far away Australia.

"As you know, I predicted this would happen. We must turn our attention and efforts to sugar cane and other crops – and for that, we'll need to find more land."

****

Jack's return from Brisbane initiates a flurry of activity. He and Duncan ride down to Nerang Heads where Jack buys a small rowing boat equipped with a mast and sail, ideal for river travel. He also buys a dog, a kelpie cross-breed, said to be good with cattle – not that Jack has any cattle yet. Nevertheless, he also buys a cow from some farmers from the Tweed. Jack sails the

101

boat back, accompanied by the dog that he names "Rusty", while Duncan rides along the riverbank, leading Polly and the cow along the slippery pathway.

"We now have some mobility!" Jack announces as he pulls the boat up on to their sandbank and tethers it to a tree.

Next, Jack and Thomasine decide to move their camp up the hill, away from possible flooding in the coming wet season, due any time from November onward. Up the hill, they set about constructing some bark huts with palm leaf roofing to replace the tents, and primitive though they are, the bark huts are a step towards a more civilised way of life.

Thomasine sets up a proper schoolroom in one of the new huts, handing out slates Jack has brought back from Brisbane for the older children to write their lessons on. Jack and his helpers cut some timber for rough school desks and benches while Thomasine opens the crates containing the books she had packed in London, and, to her dismay, she finds most of them ruined by damp and white ants.

How am I going to teach the children any British history or literature without books? she wonders. Fortunately, the children are still young enough for her to be able to impart the basics of British history from her own knowledge. However, she soon finds that stories about the kings and queens of England don't seem to interest the boys too much. May is more keen, but Thomasine decides she must consult Duncan, who, she has discovered, is surprisingly erudite in this new country where many of the inhabitants don't know how to read or write. She then invites him to come up to the hut and tell the children some tales of his time droving cattle from the Darling Downs to Sydney.

They'll pick up some Australian history that way, she decides. She also decides to get Jack to tell the boys stories of great battles in British history, which he enjoys doing.

Concerned at how hard Jack is working in the fields, often with only a handful of Aborigines, plus Edward and Roland, now seven and five, to help him when Edmund and William are away denuding the bush of its mighty cedars, Thomasine writes to her seafaring brother William to try and persuade him to come out to Queensland and work with Jack.

"If you join us and like to work for Jack we could build you a bark humpy such as we live in and Jack would allow you fifty pounds a year and single rations or else thirty pounds and double rations for yourself and wife".[1]

But William decides instead to go to Canada,[2] no doubt having long since washed his hands of his family after striking out on his own and joining the navy.

Thomasine does her best to provide tasty food for everyone, but cooking over a fire tends to limit her culinary efforts somewhat.

"We must get a fuel stove next time you go down to Nerang Heads," Thomasine tells Jack. She boils up the washing each day over the fire and tends her vegetable garden in between also tending to the needs of baby Ina and young Bertie, now an active three year old.

It isn't all work and no play, however. As the weather grows warmer, Jack decides to make a safe swimming pond for the children up near the freshwater spring where there is already a little rock pool.

"It'll keep the children safe from the sharks – not that they're man-eaters, just bullnose sharks," Jack explains. When the children aren't fishing in the river, or helping Jack, the pool becomes the centre of their activities. swimming and catching tadpoles. Rusty, the new dog, joins in all the fun and is a useful guard against snakes.

One evening in late Spring, Jack suggests to Thomasine that they should wander together up to the pond and watch the moon rise. It is a balmy night and Thomasine finds a rock to sit on while Jack strips off his clothes and plunges into the cool, dark water as the moon slowly rises above the shadowy trees.

"Tommy, it's absolutely lovely in this cool water. Why don't you take off that dress and come in?"

Thomasine hesitates. "But…I can't swim," she says, torn between her desire to try the cool water, but also timid about removing her clothes in this dark, silent bushland.

"Nobody will see you. Do come in, Tommy, you'll love it. I'll hold on to you to make sure you won't drown," Jack coaxes., "Anyway, the water's only about four feet deep."

Thomasine removes her dress and shoes and stands on the edge of the pond. Jack looks up and admires her elegant, naked figure which shows no vestige of her recent pregnancy. He stretches out his hand to her.

"Come in, darling, you look so lovely in the moonlight. Come in and I'll show you how to float – you'll love it."

As summer moves on, Thomasine and Jack return often for nocturnal swims, enjoying the sensation of some private time together at the end of their busy day.

I wonder what the parishioners of Garforth would think of me if they could see me now! Thomasine laughs to herself as she floats in the cool, moonlit water.

END NOTES CHAPTER 14

[1] Thomasine to William 1865.

[2] Where he marries Suzanna Cruise McKay. (They had 4 girls and 3 boys.) Ref: *Two Families, op cit.*

15

The Big Move

JACK AND HIS team harvest the maize and the cotton in time before the rains start. Black clouds roll over the bushland, making the dark trees loom menacingly, and flashes of lightning strike down amid torrential rain. The heat and humidity are oppressive. The river starts to rise, and, over the coming weeks, fed by its many tributaries, including the Crane Creek and Mooyumbin Creek, it swells up its banks and seeps silently upwards over their land. This flood of 1865 is a "big'un".

"And wait a year or two and there'll be another big'un."[1] Edmund warns.

By February (1866) Thomasine finds she is pregnant again. Jack is delighted and hopes for a boy.

In March, Thomasine is saddened to read a letter from her mother telling her that her brother Henry, in New Zealand, has died from tuberculosis, no doubt contracted from one of his patients. He was only 31.

In November Thomasine's seventh baby is due, and on November 11th, as with Ina, Jack delivers the baby, a boy they name Walter Alfred John, known from that moment on as either "John" or "Jack", like his father. They now have six (living) children between them and the "nursery hut" now houses two babies and a toddler.

Jack is now purchasing land about two and a half miles (4km) farther up the river, land which slopes back up to a row of hills covered with grass and light vegetation, ideal for the kind of mixed agriculture and stock he is planning. He signs the title deeds to 77 acres on January 19th 1867 for a sum of £77.15.0. He sails Thomasine up the river to show her the new land, and they decide to give it an Aboriginal name, *Ejuncum,* meaning "grassy". It will take a while to relocate their farm and to build a proper house, and Jack starts off by building a large barn – bigger than the old one at *Keith Farm* – to store their crops.

The title deeds for the land for Ejuncum

The Big Move

By March 1867 the rainy season doesn't seem to be letting up, and Jack is starting to get worried.[2] The river is already high and likely to overflow its banks soon – and life in the bark huts with the rain pouring down outside and a pack of noisy children cooped up inside is starting to wear him and Thomasine down.

Finally, Thomasine has had enough. "Jack," she says one evening, after they have struggled to cook on a fire they have finally managed to light just at the opening of the marquee that Jack has strung up outside the main hut. "I simply can't go on like this. I can't wash and dry the children's clothes, specially the nappies. I can't cook anything properly. The children are driving me mad and they don't even want to do their lessons.

"Why don't we take the plunge, literally, and sail us all up the river to the big new barn you've built at *Ejuncum* and we can live there until a proper house is built? At least we'd have more space, and a proper roof over our heads."

Jack readily agrees to this suggestion and next morning they start packing up their goods and chattels, making several boat trips up the river before packing the older boys into the boat and taking them up to the barn, leaving May to mind the infants back at *Keith Farm*. On their return, Thomasine and Jack carefully place the baby John in a packing case, and tie ropes to the hyper-active Ina and equally energetic Bertie to prevent them falling off the boat. They bid farewell to *Keith Farm* and set sail for *Ejuncum*.

April brings cooler weather, to the relief of the Browne family. But as the month wears on, the weather leading up to April 23rd becomes sultry and stormy again. On April 24th Jack sets off to check his new crops and senses a strange feeling as he walks through the bushland: there are no Aborigines flitting through the trees, no Aborigines working in his fields either. They seem to have completely disappeared.

"Where have they gone?" Thomasine asks Jack when he returns to the barn and tells her.
"I don't know," he replies, "but I'm worried. Maybe they know something we don't." On Friday 26th the rain begins in earnest and Thomasine and Jack are thankful they have decided to move the family up-river to the new barn. The rain doesn't let let up all that day and by the 27th the river is starting to swell ominously

as its already over-brimming tributaries gush their torrents into the main stream of the Nerang. Squalls of wind shake the barn and they learn later that this massive storm has hit the whole of Southern Queensland, causing such flooding of the Brisbane River that wharves are submerged. The bridge at Ipswich is swept away, trees in all areas are uprooted, and the wind lifts many houses off their foundations in Brisbane and outer townships.

By Sunday morning the Nerang River is in total flood and the Browne family is marooned in their barn. By lunchtime, the water is lapping at the door of the barn and starting to seep into the floor. Jack pulls out a ladder and climbs up into the loft where he has stored bags of potatoes for family use over the coming months. Fortunately, there are some bales of straw there too, and he pulls them open and covers part of the rough "attic" floor with it.

"Tommy, we're going to have to move everyone up here – the place is starting to flood," Jack calls down to her.

Hurriedly, as the water gushes into the barn, they carry the infants up the ladder and spread blankets out on the straw to lay the children on.

"Boys and May, start carrying up all the food – and anything else you think we'll need. Bring the jugs of fresh water with you, too," Jack commands.

With the younger children safely on the straw, Jack and Thomasine and the older children sit down on the sacks of potatoes and look at each other in amazement. The family spends the afternoon playing word games and singing songs, and from time-to-time peering down the ladder to the rising flood water.

"It looks about three feet deep," Edward observes. "I'm glad we're up here."

Thomasine makes rough sandwiches for everyone to eat and hopes their meagre supply of food will last the distance. Who knows how long they'll be stuck here in the roof of the barn?

"This is certainly the 'big'un Edmund Duncan prophesied," Jack says as the wind howls round the roof of the barn, which, thank goodness, has been sturdily built.

"It's no wonder the Aborigines have disappeared. They've been living around this river for tens of thousands of years. They'd know all the signs of a big'un."

Gradually the big storm subsides, the wind drops, the floodwaters begin to recede, and finally Thomasine and Jack carry the infants down the ladder and the older children climb back down into the barn and step out into the autumn sunshine.

"Well, this has certainly taught us a lesson," Jack declares. "We won't be building our new house down here on the flats. We'll build it right up in those hills at the back of the property!"

A month or so later, with a team of labourers up from the Tweed that Jack has hired, and some of the local Aborigines, now returned to their home, Jack starts constructing their new house: built on a "slab" of strong local timber (hence the term "slab house", raised about 18 inches (0.45 metres) above the ground to allow air to flow through it – but not as high as the later "Queenslander" houses). The house has verandas on all sides and a roof tiled with wooden shingles, two fireplaces, handsome chimneys, and floorboards fashioned from dark red cedar, perfect for the dances the Brownes will hold later on at *Ejuncum*. It's a handsome house and Thomasine and Jack are thrilled to have a proper home at last. A new stage in their lives has begun.

On August 6th 1868 Thomasine gives birth (this time with the aid of a midwife) to another daughter, Faith, meaning she now has a family of seven, ranging in age from 14 down to infancy.

END NOTES CHAPTER 15

[1] Edmund is right. The flood of 1867 will indeed be a "big'un"

[2] Extracts from: *Results of Rainfall Observations made in Queensland*, H.A. Hunt, Commonwealth Meteorologist, 1914.
http://www.bom.gov.au/qld/flood/fld_history/floodsum_1860.shtml

16

Nerang Comes of Age

MEANWHILE THERE is a stirring of activity up and down the river as word spreads to Brisbane about the rich, fertile soil on the Nerang "flats", as the semi-flood plains around the Nerang are called. Back in 1866, Jack had applied for a portion of land in what would become the Nerang township after it had been surveyed by Martin Lavelle the previous year. Jack was not alone in applying for a piece of real estate in the yet-to-be occupied town site – eight others also applied – but he pulled out before the sale, mainly because he was busily buying land for his new farming venture up the river at *Ejuncum*. This first land sale, held in Brisbane in September 1866, was a failure, with only three allotments sold (to Benjamin Bathurst of Brisbane for £7.9.0.) The failure of the sale was partly due to a financial downturn in Queensland but also to the lack of any facilities at Nerang: no post office, or any shops, or pubs, or anything, not even a gaol – and most importantly, there was no road connecting the putative town of Nerang to Brisbane.

Nevertheless, the passing of the Leasing Areas Act of 1866 encourages some intrepid settlers to apply for leases. Some other land is sold by direct auction in 1866, 1867 and 1869. Another major step in the development of Nerang is the passing in 1868 of the Crown Lands Alienation Act which leads to the resumption of vast tracts of leased Crown Lands previously occupied by William Duckett White and his son, Ernest – the earliest settlers in the district,

By the time of the second, more successful, sale in 1867, Jack's interests, and finances, have moved on. But among those who succeed in purchasing land are Jack and Thomasine's old friends, the cedar-cutters Edmund Harper and William Duncan, and another early timber cutter, Robert Veivers, who had built a bark hut at Boobigan on the Nerang back in 1861, to which he had brought his young wife, Eliza, to live. Harper purchases a 40-acre block at the junction of the Nerang River and

Tallebudgerra Creek where he builds a wharf, Harper's Wharf, which is to become a vital venue for drovers, farmers and timber cutters wanting to ship their products and cattle to Brisbane from the Nerang.

A minor Cobb & Co coach service begins in 1870 from Brisbane to Pimpama where the mail is offloaded and then taken by horseback to the Benowa post office.

By January 1871 a brand-new rough road winds through the bush from Pimpana to Nerang, and Cobb & Co start a weekly run from Brisbane to the Nerang area, stopping at Robert Muir's Benowa. Nerang now has cart and coach contact with the outside world.

In February 1871 progress on a proper road farther south from the putative Nerang township is boosted by a visit to Nerang by the Minister for Works, W.H. Walsh. Following his visit, bridges are constructed to cross the river at Tallebudgera, and at another point. [1]

With a road up to Brisbane, Nerang's prospects look up, and the Crown land sale in June 1871 is much more successful than the one Jack dropped out of back in 1867. A total of 13 allotments out of 35 offered at the sale are sold. A prominent buyer is a storekeeper from Beenleigh, James Savage, who purchases four allotments, but the biggest purchaser is Benjamin Cockerill, who buys four prime allotments and applies for the district's first publican's licence (which is granted) permitting him to open the Nerang Hotel on Robert Muir's sugar cane plantation, *Benowa*, in April 1872. The first pub in Nerang town is opened by Benjamin Cockerill in 1872; He later sells it to James Drewe. In 1873 Cockerill opens the Royal Mail Hotel on his land in Price Street, Nerang town.

However, the name Royal Mail Hotel is a slight misnomer, for the Royal Mail delivery is not to be transferred from Benowa until 1874. This proves a major problem for the two struggling Nerang township pubs because despite the fact that Cobb & Co have transferred their now thrice-weekly service from Benowa to the new Nerang township, there's still no Post Office there. The result is that not many new settlers are frequenting the pubs because picking up their mail is an important regular activity for farmers in every country town, and after they visit the Post Office, they usually end up having a few pints at the pub.

Not to be beaten by the lack of a Post Office, the two publicans decide to start the Nerang Races in an area already set aside for a racecourse by the town planners. A motley array of steeds turns up for the first race day where both publicans run booths. James Drew's *Emperor* takes the prize handicap of 12 sovereigns that first race day, and Cockerill's *Jerry* wins the one-and-a-half mile hack race valued at £6 [2] Both pubs do a roaring trade during the race meeting, and after that the Nerang Creek Races become a regular event.

Finally, on February 17th 1874, the Nerang Post Office is opened in Lenneberg's new department store. By that time, Cockerill is adding extensions to his hotel, a police barracks has been built and Nerang's first two-cell gaol is built of wood with a front veranda. Manned by Senior Constable Peter Burke, who is equipped with one horse and a bicycle, the first gaol, which is situated too close to the river, is flooded out that year and rebuilt on higher ground.

The first Nerang gaol   *The second gaol, built c1880*

The offences perpetrated by the occupants of the two gaol cells are to vary over the years from petty theft to violent assault and murder.

END NOTES CHAPTER 16

[1] Finally, in 1878, the then Premier Mr John Douglas, made the journey from Brisbane to Nerang to perform the formal opening of the first Nerang Bridge,

which was situated at the southern end of Nerang Street. The bridge was christened with a bottle of the best "Piper" (champagne) and a large procession crossed the new bridge in celebration.

[2] *Nerang Shire,* by Robert Longhurst, (Albert Shire Council, 1994.)

17

Ejuncum

The house at Ejuncum. *This photograph was taken some years after the
house was built, when the children are older. It is probable that the
woman pictured is Thomasine (her rather old-fashioned dress is
possibly one she brought out from London in 1865), and the man
holding the gun is Jack. They have obviously dressed up
for the photograph*

TO HAVE a proper house at last is thrilling for Thomasine
who has battled on for more than four years, coping with a
family of now seven children while living in first a tent and then
a bark hut. When the house is ready, they decide to go to
Brisbane to buy furniture and other items for their new abode.
As there is still no road to Brisbane, they travel there by coastal
steamer from Nerang Heads, and on their returning, their
purchases are brought up the river by one of the weekly cutters
that now ply the Nerang.

Early house guests in 1870 are Thomasine's sister, Mary,
over from New Zealand with her new husband, Robert James
Smith, having remarried after the death of her first husband,

Henry Bradley, in 1867. Now 27, she already has two sons and a daughter, and while staying at Nerang, she gives birth to Robert William, her first child by her new husband. Mary and her family move on to Stanthorpe, Queensland, and have a further two sons and six daughters. Mary and Robert will return to *Ejuncum* from time to time before they return permanently to New Zealand.

To have bedrooms for the older children and a proper nursery for the younger ones, plus a room for guests, not to mention a cookhouse for storing, preparing and cooking food, and a dining-room to which she is soon to invite some guests – for they have met some newcomers whom they find most agreeable – is more than Thomasine can dream of.

But the most thrilling thing of all is a surprise gift, sent all the way from England from Uncle Keith and his newly-wedded wife, Louisa (Jack's aunt): a piano.[1]

Sitting down to play her favourite Schubert melodies at her own piano, in her own house, looking out over the green hills to their farmland makes Thomasine happier than she has ever been. She starts teaching May how to play, reminding her that she had begun music lessons with her back in London. The boys are less keen, but they enjoy joining with Jack and singing around the piano.

"We're going to live like civilised British people from now on," Thomasine tells the family. "This means everybody must take off their muddy shoes and boots before stepping inside the house – and we'll all dress for dinner every evening."

A far-flung post of the British Empire is thus established at *Ejuncum*.

****

Thomasine and Jack, being naturally convivial, begin to befriend their neighbours who are starting to settle nearby. Jack's warm smile and ability to set broken bones and heal wounds, and his willingness to lend anyone a hand around their property, soon help him to make new friends in the district, while Thomasine always has a welcoming cup of tea ready for anyone who calls in at *Ejuncum*. As Jack says: "Tommy, you've now started to have another Stoke Prior here on the Nerang."

In August 1870 Thomasine is pregnant again, this time with twins. "I'm living up to my name: 'Thomasine' means 'twins'!"

But tragedy is to follow when, in April 1871, she gives birth to the twins, a boy and a girl. Sadly, the boy, William Ernest, lingers on for nine days after birth but the girl twin, Jessie, dies at birth. Thomasine then quickly becomes pregnant again and gives birth prematurely on December 27th to another baby, a girl, who is stillborn.[2] Although, as a Victorian woman, she is accustomed to deaths of babies – and mothers – in childbirth, Thomasine grieves at the loss of her twins and the unnamed stillborn baby, but by February of the following year, 1872, she is pregnant again – her 12th pregnancy – and gives birth in October to another daughter, Ada Maude.

As there is still no school at Nerang, Thomasine expands her classroom at *Ejuncum* to fit not only her own growing brood, but also the sons and daughters of the local farmers who are moving into the area. She is also teaching some of these children to play the piano.

Jack and Thomasine make particular friends with a fellow pioneer settler, Henry Schneider, who, despite his German surname, is third-generation English and bridles when the authorities insist on naming him "Heinrich" Schneider on the title of the land he purchases when he joins another fellow expat Oxford student, John D'Oyley Hutchins, in a cotton-growing venture, the *Gilston* plantation on the Nerang River in 1866.

Henry Schneider, the son of a Lincolnshire clergyman, has graduated with a B.A. from Trinity College, Oxford in 1865, and perhaps lured by Hutchins, almost immediately set sail for Queensland. He loved singing, having been a chorister at Magdalen, Oxford, from the age of 11 to 15, and he is soon accompanying Thomasine on the piano, together with Jack, in musical sessions at *Ejuncum*. Whenever he comes, Henry asks May to join in the singing, and Thomasine soon notes that the two of them are getting along together very well.

Henry Schneider's *Gilston* planation, blessed by the frequent rains in the Nerang district which stave off the drought which has plagued other parts of southern Queensland, produces good crops of cotton, However, along with two other Oxford graduates, William and Charles Philpott (William was a fellow chorister with Henry at Magdalen), Henry is to take over *Gilston* from John D'Oyley, changing its name to *Birribi,* and switching to sugar cane farming and, with the help of Robert Muri, they set up an early sugar mill.

Henry Schneider and the Philpotts are examples of successful settlers in these early days when many other would-be settlers fail because the apparently dry land they have bought turns out to become a complete swamp most of the year after the rains start. Others try their hand at cotton or sugar cane but aren't up to the struggle of farming in this hot, humid, weed-and-insect-infested area with no machinery and only horses available for ploughing. Nevertheless, those who stick at it – like Jack, Henry Schneider, the Philpott brothers, Robert Muir, and Stephen Tobin of the nearby township of Tallebudgera, succeed and prosper – and some of the land they have purchased will later turn out to be worth large sums as Surfers Paradise emerges from the farmland.

By late 1872, Jack is finding the location of *Ejuncum* up in the hills, away from the river, becoming irksome. Not only does he often have to ride back-and-forth up to the house several times a day on various errands, but also visitors arriving by boat find the walk from the river to the house wearing, especially when it is raining – which it does very heavily during the wet season.

When cockatoos begin invading his crops Jack has to take Edward and Roland on the back of his horse each morning down to the paddock where they have to spend the day frightening off, with loud banging of pots and pans, the sulphur-crested white birds which come in great waves of flapping and cawing with marauding zeal. Having to isolate the two boys for so many hours a day worries Jack and he finally comes to a decision:

"Tommy, we're going to have to move the house down closer to the river," he tells Thomasine. "The house is too far away from the working farm and it's not fair on Edward and Roland to have to spend their days isolated in that field. I've checked and re-checked the water levels during periods of flooding, and I've consulted the Aborigines, and I now know where it would be safe to relocate the house.

"We'll simply take it to pieces, bit by bit, and cart it down closer to the river and rebuild it."

"But where will we live while that's happening?" asks Thomasine, rather taken aback by Jack's resolve.

"While the house is being rebuilt we'll just have to live in the barn, like we did during the flood, It won't take long – just a couple of weeks."

Thomasine, thankfully not pregnant at the time, agrees. She, too, can see the advantages of moving down closer to the river, particularly as the older children can now sail a boat. The rebuilding proceeds smoothly and the house is soon ready. Being located closer to the farmland and the river suits all the family and Jack widens his holding, as Lena Cooper relates:

> "Now it was more convenient to work the farm, more trees were felled till there was 30 acres under cultivation. Cotton, maize, potatoes, sugar cane and a small patch of arrowroot were grown. Mrs Browne saw that there were plenty of fruit trees besides cape gooseberries, passionfruit and tomatoes which grew wild."[3]

After getting *Ejuncum*'s kitchen set up, Thomasine takes on an Aboriginal couple whom she calls "Joe" and "Annie:" because their native names are too difficult for her European ears. From time-to-time Joe and Annie bring their relatives to help when animals are being slaughtered for the storeroom. Thomasine finds them amiable workers, although inclined to wander off with their tribe from time to time. She busies herself organising her first dinner party at their new address early in 1874.

With her dinner guests invited, Thomasine prepares for the party. She teaches Joe and Annie how to set a dinner table, and how to serve the food. She has invited Henry Schneider, the Philpotts and Robert Muir. And with May and Edward, the big table comfortably seats eight. Jack offers them sherry and they stand around the piano and sing, before sitting down to the meal.

Their guests are impressed by the freshly-starched white tablecloth, the sparkling glasses which Thomasine and Jack have brought out of storage in Brisbane, and the gleaming silver, plus the red native bottlebrush blooms in a vase which give an Australian touch to the table. Jack raises his glass: "To our dear Queen Victoria, may God bless her." Thomasine remarks that the widowed Queen's family is now almost all grown up. "The youngest, Princess Beatrice, must be 16 by now. Our Queen has had nine children – I've more than equalled her with my nine living children!" They settle down happily to a delicious soup served from a large silver tureen, and the conversation, too, sparkles.

They begin by discussing the changes coming to Nerang now that there's a road to Brisbane and Cobb & Co have based a staging post in Nerang to and from Brisbane. They hope that will liven up things in the infant town. "We still only have two pubs in it – and nothing else!" Jack exclaims. "But the Cobb & Co coaches going to Brisbane will make all the difference."

"I was impressed by the way those two pub owners organised the first Nerang Races over two years ago to entice some customers into the town," Henry Schneider says, "But, Jack, remember we've now also got Lennebergs' department store, and the Post Office will be set up in Nerang township early next year!"

The conversation then turns to sugar cane farming. "I see that Price's old estate now has 75 acres under cane," William Philpott comments, "and they're employing quite a few South Sea Islanders there, too."

He adds "we've now got 40 acres of cane at *Birribi.*"

Thomasine then calls in Joe and Annie to remove the soup plates and bring in the main course of roast lamb.

As Joe and Annie come into the dining room and start clearing the plates, Thomasine observes startled looks on her guests' faces, and stifled snorts behind napkins. Her guests are looking, goggle-eyed at Joe and Annie, who are stark naked. Being ladies and gentlemen, her guests then compose themselves and turn a polite blind eye to the state of undress of the servants. But afterwards, Thomasine confesses her embarrassment to Jack: "I'm mortified! I'm so used to the

Aborigines' dangly bits, I completely forgot they were naked!" she says. "I'll have to run up some garments for them to wear when we're having dinner in future. And anyway, the girls are growing up now and they should be shielded from such things."[4]

So next day, Thomasine rummages in a cupboard and pulls out a bale of red flannel she had brought out from England to make nightclothes for the children, unaware that the climate on the Nerang would be so hot and humid – totally unsuitable for red flannel, so she had stored it away. Now, forgetting her reason for not using the flannel, she decides to make use of it and sits down at her trusty sewing machine and starts running up some long red flannel shirts for Joe and Annie.

Jack remonstrates with her: "Tommy darling, I don't think red flannel shirts will go down too well with the Aborigines. It's far too hot – and they have their pride. You must admit that red flannel shirts will look ridiculous on them."

But Thomasine perseveres and her native kitchen staff reluctantly don their new garb, and, with sulky expressions, they serve dinner for the family that night. To Thomasine's dismay, however, after dinner a mighty tribal brawl erupts in the yard outside and the red flannel shirts get short shrift and are torn to shreds. After that, Thomasine manages to persuade Joe and Annie to wear pieces of curtain material she gives them as loincloths, and the matter is settled.

****

Thomasine's home school is expanding fast with more and more local children joining in her classes, and, pregnant once more, she is beginning to find coping with the educational needs of 24 children ranging in age from five to 16 something of a burden. "I'll be glad when they finally set up a proper school," she tells Jack. "Then perhaps I'll find a little more time to try and civilise Ina."

Ina, now nine, has grown into a very pretty, wilful, hyper-energetic little red-headed tomboy, playing out in the stream next to *Ejuncum* with the local boys and outdoing them in exploits of daring and feats of stupidity – so much so that one day she falls from a tree branch into a shallow pool and cuts her face on a rock.

This is the last straw for Thomasine, who drags the blood-spattered girl back into the house, cleans up her face, and then sits her down in front of a mirror on the bedroom wall.

"Now Ina, you are going to sit there until lunchtime and you're going to look at that face of yours in the looking-glass. I want you to realise that your face will be your chief asset in life. A girl must look as beautiful as possible in order to catch a suitable husband. That face of yours is your passport to a comfortable world."

Ina, squirming, sits in front of the mirror for three hours, staring at her face, but this draconian treatment does little to curtail her wild antics.

"I can only hope and pray she'll knuckle down to her lessons when she starts school," Thomasine says.

****

A sad family event occurs in March 1874. Thomasine and Jack learn of the death of their old friend and benefactor, Sir William Keith Ball, at the age of 83, leaving his widow, Louisa, as heir to much of his estate.

Thomasine has mixed feelings at hearing this news: *Poor dear Keith. I owe him so much. He was buried at the Holy Trinity Churchyard in West Sussex,* she muses. *If I'd married him I would have been at his graveside, like Louisa was. I was very fond of Keith but I must admit I made the right decision to marry Jack and come to Australia!*

That month, too, Thomasine gives birth to a second set of twins – girls – both of whom die at birth, leaving her suffering deep post-natal depression.[5]

I simply can't go on bringing these little mites into the world only to have them die, she thinks as she wanders aimlessly around the house, unable to summon her customary energy to do anything.

One afternoon, a fortnight after the birth, she reaches a trough of despair as she waits for Jack to ride home from his farming. As she hears his horse's hoofs pounding the driveway, she goes out to the front door and flings herself down over the threshold.

"Ride over me with your horse, Jack, and put me out of my misery!" she screams.

On hearing this pitiful cry, Jack hastily dismounts and tethers his horse to the veranda post and rushes to Thomasine.

"Tommy, my darling, darling Tommy," he says, holding her close. "We simply can't let you suffer any longer. You've already had 13 babies, and nine are alive and well. What can we do?"

He carries her into the bedroom, and they lie together with Thomasine quietly sobbing.

"Well," she finally says, "I'm 42 now, so I'm unlikely to go on having too many more babies. I can't think of anything that can be done, short of never sharing a bed with you again – and I couldn't bear that!"

"Tommy, I love you dearly," Jack comforts her. "I couldn't bear the thought of not having you in my bed either!"

So they let the matter rest for a while until Thomasine's sister Mary comes for a visit in October 1875. By that time, Mary and her husband and growing family are living in Stanthorpe, Queensland, where Robert, formerly a storekeeper in New Zealand, has become a gold miner. [6].

Thomasine, restored by now to her former self, and soon to be pregnant yet again, sits down at the kitchen table over a cup of tea with Mary and pours out her problem to her:

"I love Jack, and all my children dearly," Thomasine begins, "But I simply can't go on being with child so much of the time."

Mary then tells her what she knows about methods of preventing conception. In those Victorian days, the options are limited, and not pleasant – nor are they particularly effective.

"I read in *The Lady* magazine about what they call "Womb Veils," Mary says, "Apparently, they're little pockets of muslin about an inch square which a woman can stuff with anything, even a slice of lemon. But most women stuff more muslin into the pocket to make a sponge and they soak it in brandy or lemon juice. Then they tie the pocket with a long silk string and insert it into themselves with the string hanging out so the pocket can be pulled back out later."

"That sounds most uncomfortable! "Thomasine exclaims. "Have you tried it?"

"No," Mary replies. "I'm quite happy with my babes at the moment. But later on, maybe…"[7]

"Is there any other solution?" Thomasine asks.

"Well, there are things the husband can put on, made of thick rubber or from animal intestines. They're said to be very uncomfortable for both the husband and the wife. I've heard that someone[8] in America has invented a new kind of soft rubber and that the devices made from it are much better. But I haven't heard they're available yet in Australia."

END NOTES CHAPTER 17

[1] Thousands of pianos were shipped to Australia in the 19th century, leading to claims that there were more pianos per head of population than in any other country.

[2] This pregnancy probably occurred so soon after the death of the newborn twins because Thomasine wasn't breastfeeding which very often inhibited conception.

[3] *Two Families*, op cit.

[4] *Two Families* op cit.

[5] The birth is incorrectly listed in *Ancestry* as just one child.

[6] They finally return to New Zealand in 1885.

[7] Mary is to go on to have 11 children.

[8] Charles Goodyear invented the vulcanisation of rubber in 1839, with the first rubber condoms appearing in 1844 which were gradually adopted, first in the USA, and later on, worldwide.

18

School

THE YEAR 1875 sees Nerang begin to blossom. After a severe flood in March that year, the newly-built Police Barracks and Court of Petty Sessions suffer in the severe floods and it is decided they must be moved to safer ground as soon as possible. Meanwhile, the town now sports a butcher, saddler, baker, and bootmaker. Benjamin Cockerill has successfully opened his Royal Mail Hotel in Price Street and the Nerang Christmas races have now become a fixture.

But Nerang is not the only riverside town which is starting to grow; Tallebuggera, sensitive to its burgeoning status now it has its own regular horse race, and first accommodation house (opened by Stephen Tobin), officially changes its name to Tallebudgera. Indeed, Tallebudgera is starting to leave the town of Nerang behind in its rapid development.

Another step in the area's development is the first official survey of Nerang Heads by G. L. Pratten, which leads to the area being re-named Southport[1] and soon to become a booming resort town for the better-off Brisbane citizens, and the Nerang locals, including Thomasine and Jack and their friends, who join in. and sometimes lead, a range of social activities in coming years.

At last, on November 1st, 1875 the Nerang School opens. It was built by James Phillips at a cost of £378. Jack, who has worked hard to establish the school, is its first Chairman, with Thomas Johnson its first headmaster and teacher.[2] The older boy pupils are allowed time off from their schoolwork to help during sowing and harvesting, while the older girls are given one day off a week from school to help their mothers with the baking.

Thomasine is fervently thankful the school is finally open. Young Ina, now ten, in particular, needs some disciplining. "Ina is completely out of control," Thomasine tells the new schoolmaster. "She's very bright but extremely wilful and she's been running wild all her young life. My other children all behave themselves, but not our Ina. I hope attending a proper school will sort her out."

The first Nerang school

The children either ride horses or sail up the river to the school, a whole world opening up to them with new friendships and fresh ideas to sharpen their rustic minds – and, cooped up all day in classrooms, they fall prey to all the usual childhood ailments: measles, mumps and chickenpox, but thankfully not diphtheria.

With the opening of the school, a new horizon also opens for Thomasine when Jack suggests she should learn to ride again.

"You'd be able to ride out to some of the outlying properties to teach the children music," he suggests, and Thomasine eagerly agrees to the idea. Jack selects a young but reliable mare for her, and riding lessons begin. Thomasine decides to call her horse Maisie and she remembers some of the riding skills her father, Michael, had taught her all those years ago at Tring. However, as she soon finds herself with child again, riding becomes difficult and her plan to ride out to teach music is postponed until after the birth, which is due in early July 1876.

As the date of birth draws near, Jack suggests that because of the danger of yet another stillbirth, she should go to Brisbane this time where she can have good hospital care. Thomasine agrees and sets off by coach for the arduous and bumpy nine-hour journey to Brisbane, which she and the unborn baby happily survive. Jack later rides to Brisbane to join her for the birth.

On July 2nd 1876 Thomasine, now aged 43, is delivered of a son. The birth is difficult, and Thomasine has to remain in hospital for a week or two. Jack decides to take matters into his own hands, telling Thomasine he thinks the best plan is for him to take the baby back to Nerang while she recovers in Brisbane. With some trepidation, Thomasine agrees to this plan; the thought of having to take a young baby back on that nine-hour coach journey doesn't appeal to her.

"I'll get him straight onto cow's milk," Jack promises, "May will love to help look after him till you get back."

And so, a week after the baby is born, Jack straps the infant into a sling under his arm and rides off to Nerang on his powerful stallion, Rupe. Jumping every fence on the way back with customary aplomb, Jack cries out "Up me Barney Brannigan!" [3] They arrive at *Ejuncum* safely, and when Thomasine returns home, they christen the baby Lionel Edgar, but the child is always known as "Barney".

****

By now, much of the labour in the Nerang canefields – and all over the Queensland cane-growing regions – is carried out by indentured South Sea Island labour[4]. This is particularly the case in the Nerang area on the big estates, such as Price's old 75-acre cane estate (now owned by Holland Miskin and Co) and Thomasine and Jack's friends, Henry Schneider and brothers William and Charles Philpott's *Birribi* 40-acre plantation on Mooyumbin Creek. Such estates habitually employ around 60 or so "Kanakas"[5], some of whom choose to extend their stays beyond the allotted time of three years.

Thomasine's eldest son, Edward, is later to employ South Sea Island labour too, after he buys *Keith Farm* from Jack and starts growing sugar cane there.

As early as 1860 (see Appendix B) a few South Sea Islanders had come to Queensland to work in the *beche de mer* industry. The early cane field owners realised these Islanders, coming as they did from tropical climes, were ideal for working in the hot, humid Queensland cotton and cane districts. The first major shipment of 67 South Sea Islanders arrived at Moreton Bay in 1863 on board the *Don Juan*, coming to work on Townes' cotton plantation on the Logan River. They were the first of approximately 60,000 indentured South Sea Islanders to come to Australia over the years up to the early 20th Century. As cotton became surpassed by sugar cane, most of them worked in the canefields, although some worked in other agricultural pursuits and a few ended up in domestic service.

Over the years, starting with the Pacific Labourers Act of 1868, the Queensland Government[6] endeavoured to deal with the problems of employing these workers from the Solomon Islands, the New Hebrides, Vanuatu, New Caledonia, and later on, New Guinea and the archipelago of islands to its east, though others came from the Loyalty Islands. Early government legislation endeavoured to stamp out the evil practice of "blackbirding" or kidnapping islanders and bringing them to Australia as virtual slaves.

The Queensland Government's attempts to grapple with the problems of the influx of South Sea Islanders was given a boost in 1873 with the proclamation of the Electoral Districts Act and the subsequent election of Philip Henry Nind as the representative of the Logan District. Nind was an advocate of South Sea Island labour and worked to improve their conditions.

Later legislation dealt with the need to establish reasonable work practices, living conditions, and a wage structure. Many plantation owners in Queensland complied with the Government's rules and treated their workers well, but some did not. It was difficult to check on the treatment of workers in outlying districts and many stories of ill-treatment prevailed, giving rise to the term "sugar slaves" to describe those who suffered cruelty, On the other hand, many islanders queued up to come to work in Australia after they observed the bounty their older brothers and a few sisters brought back at the end of their time on the canefields. Indeed, despite modern condemnation of "blackbirding", many Islanders chose to make return visits to work in Australia.

The entire practice of employing South Sea Island labour ends in an iniquitous manner when the newly-constituted Federal Government (inaugurated in 1901), influenced by the Union movement, enacts "The White Australia Policy" and carries out the forced eviction –"repatriation" – of most of the Islanders, legislating that only European or "white" labour is to be employed from that period on.

****

A new friend swims – or rather, punts – into Thomasine and Jack's circle when a friend of Henry Schneider, a fellow surveyor, steps off his small boat onto the jetty at *Ejuncum*, and, walking across the lawn, introduces himself to Jack.

"My name is John Brown," he says, shaking Jack's welcoming hand. "Brown with **no** 'e'," he adds.

"And my name's John Browne **with** an 'e' – Walter John Browne – but call me Jack," says Jack, laughing.

From that moment on, John Brown, a mild-mannered, highly-cultured bachelor three years older than Thomasine, becomes part of the *Ejuncum* scene, visiting frequently although based in Brisbane, where he lives with his musically talented twin sister, Louisa Ann[7], who was widowed in Sydney in 1872. John's father was John Goldfinch Brown, a wealthy coal broker and warehouse owner from Wapping in London, who (according to family lore) lost all his money in a disastrous warehouse fire for which he unfortunately wasn't insured.[8] This led to his wife and younger children, including John and his sister Louisa, and her husband, James Wilks and daughter, Constance, migrating to Australia. After James Wilks dies at the age of 44 in 1872, Louisa and Constance move to Brisbane to join her brother John. Constance then dies, aged only 21. Louisa then continues to run her brother's household. Now happily settled in Brisbane and working as a surveyor and conveyancer for one of the two leading legal firms in Brisbane, John Brown is also busily investing in real estate there and moving up in Queensland government circles to eventually become Deputy Registrar of Title. After his initial meeting with the Nerang Brownes, he is a regular visitor and gets on well with Thomasine and Jack, becoming almost a member of the family.

****

In February 1876 the Eastern Extension Company lays telegraph cable between La Perouse, New South Wales, and Wakapuaka near Nelson, NZ. The New South Wales and New Zealand governments subsidise the cost. Connections overland via Adelaide and Darwin, and undersea via Java and Suez, allow telegraphic contact with London that same year. World events in 1876 are now reaching Brisbane almost instantly and news of mounting European tensions leads to a growing fear of invasion of the colonies of Queensland and New South Wales. The colonial Governors seek advice from Lt. General Jervois on their fortifications, artillery, naval defences and manoeuvres.

News also reaches Nerang of Queen Victoria's new title of Empress of India, which was bestowed on May 1, 1876,[9] Jack pricks up his ears at this development and immediately recalls, his happy days in India with the British Army under the raj. This inspires him to join in the military-style activity which is starting up in Southport.

The following year, 1877 Henry Schneider decides to give up his shareholding in the sugar cane plantation at *Birribi* and sets off to the Roma district accompanied by young Edward Cooper where they demonstrated their cane threshing machine to the local farmers there. They return in time for Christmas that year, when Henry resumes his interest in young May Cooper, now aged 21.

Thomasine and Jack in a formal pose, 1877

In October 1877 Thomasine gives birth to her last child, a daughter, Rosamond Alice. Thomasine, now 44, has decided to have the birth at Nerang, assisted by a local midwife.

"My last child," she declares, "and a healthy one too, thank God."

As soon as the baby is weaned and a nursemaid hired from Brisbane is put in charge of the *Ejuncum* nursery, Thomasine breathes a sigh of relief, free now at last to improve her riding skills to ready herself to ride out through the bush to outlying properties to teach the children there how to play the piano.

"Tommy, I know you're now a very competent horsewoman – after all, I've trained you, but you'll find yourself riding through some dangerous terrain at times," Jack warns her. "Many of the outlying farms still don't have proper road access – they're still relying on the river and creeks for getting around.

So you'll find yourself picking your way through dense bush, maybe deep mud, with perhaps only a rough track to follow, and possibly fallen trees barring your way.

"I'm worried about you venturing out like this, all on your own."

But Thomasine is adamant: "Jack, I really want to do something to help these children," she insists. "They're living such a very long way from any civilisation. And for my part, I've been stuck in the house for too long. I'll be very careful. But I think I might resort to wearing a pair of the older boys' riding breeches in case I have to dismount and cut my way through the bush and jungle, and I'll just dismount and change into a skirt when I'm close to my destination."

"Well, at least we now have a bridge over the River," Jack concedes, realising that once Thomasine has set her mind on a plan there's no way of stopping her, "so you won't have to get your horse to wade through the water." He's referring to the first bridge over the Nerang, which was opened on December 7th 1778, by the Premier, the Hon. John Douglass.

Able now to cross the Nerang River without getting wet, Thomasine intrepidly sets off on Maisie once a week, riding as far as the Binsteads and the Howards at Upper Coomera to give piano lessons to the young daughters of the property owners there.

Thomasine also now has time to help Jack, the Philpott brothers, Henry Schneider, and other members of the Nerang community[10] with the establishment of Nerang's first church, St. Margaret's Church of England, which opens on January 29th 1878, with the Rev. John Gilberton holding monthly services. Thomasine is appointed the church organist – as she had been all those years ago at Hawes in Yorkshire – and she also starts teaching Nerang children how to play the organ.

The first wedding at St Margaret's is on April 3rd 1879, when Henry Schneider and Thomasine's eldest daughter, May, tie the knot. After their marriage the newly-weds go to the Mackay district to further demonstrate Henry's sugar-making machinery. After the birth of their first daughter, they go to live in Prince Street, Nerang, while Henry develops his surveying career. Over the coming years, Henry Schneider, who is a foundation member of the Queensland Surveyors' Institute, is to survey much of the area which is to become the Gold Coast, particularly Coolangatta. Not long after they move to Prince Street, the Schneiders start building a house on the bank of the river, which they name *Umpinido*.

Thomasine and Jack's family get-togethers continue apace at *Ejuncum* with neighbours joining in. On one occasion when their old friends and neighbours, the Hutchins, go to the Brownes, the two ladies have a running race on the lawn near the jetty and it is reported that "Mrs Browne, though much older than Mrs Hutchins, won the race". [11].

****

By the late 1870s Southport, with its boarding houses and hotels, has become a popular tourist destination. People often travel to Nerang from Brisbane by the now thrice-weekly Cobb & Co then take the recently established Meyer's ferry service down the Nerang River to Southport, especially for the Southport Easter Regatta which has just been inaugurated.

Thomasine, Jack, the Philpotts and Henry Schneider find themselves travelling down to Southport more regularly to take part in sporting and social activities. (Henry Schneider, who had won a pair of silver oars at Cambridge as a sculling trophy, coaches the Cooper brothers – Edward and Roland – in rowing, and in 1879 all three win a silver cup at the Southport Regatta. Thomasine and Jack are leading lights in these social activities where other "movers and shakers" in the district meet to discuss the formation of a system of local government and associations – the Agricultural and Pastoralists Association being an important example – which will start full operations in the early 1880s. Jack is to be a leading figure in these activities.

Even though Southport is now becoming a hive of tourist and trading activity[12], Nerang and the other Nerang River area towns like Tallebudgera (where a school and church have now been built and a cricket club and racecourse have opened) are moving ahead. More new settlers are coming into Nerang now the Mission reserve for Aborigines has been closed and is opened to farmers keen to exploit the rich, fertile land of that part of the Nerang "flats". Joint district events bring everyone together for regular district ploughing matches, and a combined team of Nerang, Coomera and Tallebudgera cricketers meet and sometimes battle against a Brisbane team.[12]

To an outsider, such socialising must have seemed very similar to the social scene in rural England. But there is a big difference: these pioneers are not all from the English upper middle class, nor are they snobs. Sugar cane farmers and cattle breeders and hotel owners and storekeepers in southern Queensland in the 19th Century – as farming people all over country Australia – come from all kinds of backgrounds and walks of life. The old English class system is withering away in this new country where everyone relies on everyone else for help, friendship and support. These early settlers, enjoying their cricket and racing and regattas after long battles with floods and droughts, marauding insects, isolation and loneliness and, often, financial struggles, are the forerunners of the egalitarian qualities which characterise Australians to this day.

END NOTES CHAPTER 18

[1] The population of Southport in 1875 is 30; Coolangatta is 14, and Burleigh Heads, 8. The first house in Southport is built in 1877 by Robert Johnson and his son, Ralph.

[2] Some of the 47 first pupils include six of Thomasine's children: Edward, Roland, and Herbert "Bertie" Cooper; Thomasina (Ina), John and Faith Browne. Other pupils include Alice, Christina, Adelaide, Sarah, Arthur and Julia Batten; James and Elizabeth Ross; George, Dolly and Dinah Cockerill; Arthur and Eliza Warples; John and Horace Johnston; Henrietta and Matilda Karkow; James and Cissie Thompson; Mary, Martha, Rose, Matthew and William Hope; John, Robert and Jessie Veivers; Charles, Frederick, Annie and Augusta Berg; William and Henry Gooding; Ada Cockerill; Matthew Muir; and James Mitchell.(Ref: *Nerang Shire.*)

[3] Name of a popular Irish drinking song revived in more recent times.

[4] Refs: *SUGAROPOLIS Journeys to The Australian South Sea Islands Story of the Gold Coast Region*
http://www.goldcoast.qld.gov.au/documents/bf/history-south-sea-islanders-booklet.pdf

Sugar Slaves by Imelda Miller https://www.qhatlas.com.au/content/sugar-slaves

[5] The word "Kanaka" originally referred only to native Hawaiians, from their own name for themselves, *kānaka 'ōiwi* or *kānaka maoli*. Eventually, it was applied to all South Sea Islanders, no matter which island they came from. The name "Kanaka" is today regarded as offensive by many people in Australia.

[6] See Appendix B.

[7] Louisa arranged musical events at Government House, Brisbane.

[8] Cousin Genevieve Grainger queries this, saying: "I'd be interested to know where this info comes from re the fire. In the National Archives John Goldfinch Brown is frequently listed with his insurance policies on properties, from memory in Horseferry Rd and Commercial Rd.
He spoke for the need of securing the barges in the Thames, carrying coal, that were often robbed at night, losing overall perhaps a million pounds a year. He promoted the establishment of a Water Police Force. So he was well aware of safety and protection of property.". [Author's note: John would have inherited a very prosperous enterprise, then why did he instead emigrate to Brisbane?]

[9] The new title was proclaimed at the Delhi Durbar of January 1st 1877.

[10] *Nerang Shire*, p67.

[11] *Two Families, op cit.*, p15

[12] Lena Cooper's manuscript, *op cit.*

19

The Booming 1880s

THE 1880s are to be boom years for the Nerang and Southport areas – and much of the rest of Queensland.
The first annual Nerang Races are held on January 1st 1880. A fitting start to a new decade," Jack declares, as Thomasine and the family spread a rug on the turf beside the somewhat makeshift temporary racetrack in Viever's paddocks. Soon neighbours arrive from up and down the river and refreshments, and bets, start to flow. There's a feeling of optimism among the people of Nerang – an optimism which is to blossom during the coming decade as the revenue from sugar cane, timber, dairy farming and tourism starts to swell the pockets of so many of the pioneers who have survived the floods and the bugs and beetles and the grinding effort to get their farms productive. There's much talk about the newly-formed Nerang Divisions Board, set up by the Queensland Government to push the locals to look after their own new roads, bridges and other works for which the State had previously held responsibility.

Jack is to be the Board's first Chairman, a role for which he is ideally suited, and the first meeting of the Board is on February 19th 1880. The first Board consists of three Divisions:

1.   The north side of Nerang and Southport
2.   The south side of Nerang and Mudgeeraba
3.   Tallebudgera and Currumbin

It doesn't take long for Southport to clamour for its own Division, claiming it urgently needs a proper sea wall to be built, and a sizeable jetty to cope with the ever-increasing number of tourist vessels arriving from Brisbane, not to mention other facilities which a booming seaside holiday town requires. As Southport is providing the bulk of the revenue for Division 1, its supporters start claiming all Division 1's funds are being spent on culverts and gutters and drains in and around Nerang township, which is regarded as "a sleepy English hollow" compared to bustling Southport. By 1883 the townspeople of Southport get their way and Southport is granted its own Board.

Nerang may be "sleepy", but many of its residents, such as Jack, Thomasine, the Philpott brothers and Lennenburg (who, admittedly, finally moves his store to Southport), are not only persevering with their farming and other projects but are also leading lights in the various sporting activities in and beyond Nerang, such as the cricket matches and ploughing matches, and the newly-formed Annual Southport Regatta.

The men aren't the only ones involved in local politics, either – the women play an important, though behind-the-scenes role too. Victorian ladies aren't often involved in direct politics, nevertheless they have a profound influence, introducing important newcomers to the older denizens of the emerging Gold Coast area, sorting out arguments and disputes between families, as well as often playing the role of hostess and arranging events such as the Southport Regatta Ball.

Thomasine is particularly adept at "behind the scenes" manoeuvres and she knows from Jack everything that is going on in the new Division Boards, such as the jockeying for positions, or the reason why early Nerang storekeeper H.G. Bryant resigns as its first Auditor and why William Philpott takes over, and she's also happy to gossip with the ladies over the latest dress fashion, the bustle, which is re-emerging with a vengeance, as the style of dress for the 1880s.

20

A Frightening Storm and
a Stormy Daughter

"I CAN'T IMAGINE how a lady can possibly even think of riding a horse when she's wearing a bustle," Thomasine jokes to Jack as he helps her to mount Maisie, who is now getting a trifle elderly, but is still a sturdy mount.

It's a sizzling January morning as Thomasine prepares to set off through the bush to teach music to the girls in a family living on an isolated farm about a three-hour ride from *Ejuncum* on the northern side of the river.

"I'm glad I'm flouting convention wearing my riding breeches," she adds. "I've become completely accustomed to changing into a dress in the scrub before I reach my pupils."

"Well," says Jack, checking her stirrups. "Off you go, but be careful to check the weather before you return. We might be in for another big thunderstorm today."

"I'll take care," Thomasine promises. "I'll even stay at their homestead overnight if the weather looks too threatening."

With that, Thomasine sets off across the ever-more rickety Nerang bridge and into the thick jungle bushland. The cicadas are at full throttle and a hot sun beats down from a cloudless sky. The bush is heating up already, flies hover over Maisie, and Thomasine pushes on for an hour until a fallen log blocks the track ahead.

"Well, Maisie, let's jump it," Thomasine says, clamping her knees against her horse and landing neatly on the other side. "Time to find some water for you now," she adds, leading Maisie to a nearby stream. Thomasine sits on a log and looks up at the sky high above the bamboo and tall eucalypts. A flock of lorikeets soars over, screeching, and she can hear a rustling in the undergrowth; a bush rat, probably.

They press on, and an hour or so later, reach the farmhouse where the family welcomes her with a cup of tea and cake on the wide veranda before the music lessons begin. After lunch

Thomasine holds some more lessons with the younger children, and at 3.30 pm she looks out the window and observes the clouds mounting in the formerly clear sky. The calls of currawongs echo through the suddenly still air – a sure sign of rain and a storm ahead.

I'd better set off home, now, she decides, *I don't really want to stay here overnight.*

Bidding farewell to her students and their parents, Thomasine and Maisie set off into the bush. The storm clouds are now looming, and Thomasine is worried. *I hope I'll manage to get back home in time,* she thinks as she pushes Maisie into a trot and then a canter as they follow the fairly well-made section of the track leading from the farm. As she rides deeper into the bush, Thomasine is forced to slow Maisie down. The track is very muddy in parts, due to the previous night's storm, and she can now hear faint rumbles of thunder coming through the ever-darkening clouds. *Well, we've gone too far to turn back now,* she tells Maisie after riding for almost half an hour.

She peers up at the darkening sky where scuds of cockatoos are swirling high above. A small pack of startled wallabies hop across the track in front of her, searching for shelter. Then the rain starts to spatter. Dismounting to get her wet-weather jacket out of her travelling bag, Thomasine pats Maisie on her neck and remounts. *I'll just have to keep my head down and push on,* she decides. About an hour goes by and she still has yet another hour or more of riding before her. The thunder is now augmented by flashes of lightning and sudden cracks of thunder. The track has become ever more sodden with this new rain and Thomasine and Maisie are now slowly plodding almost to a halt. A wild wind starts to howl through the trees and the heavy rain turns into a massive downpour. Lightning strikes a tree in front of them, stopping them in their tracks as the tree trunk bursts into flames. Thomasine is quite accustomed to lightning striking trees – the tall tree in front of *Ejuncum* has been struck, bursting into flames, on several occasions.[1]

By now, Thomasine is seriously worried. *Maybe I had better turn off this quagmire of a track and get down to the river where I can follow the track along the bank,* she decides, turning her frightened steed down towards the river. *At least I'll know I'm going in the right direction.* The rain is pelting down and Thomasine is drenched to the skin despite her wet-weather clothing. The water has seeped into her boots too. *At least the temperature is warm,* she thinks, her mind flashing back briefly to her time in Yorkshire travelling around the parish in the cold rain. *I shan't freeze in this semi-tropical climate.* The lightning and thunder are now even more fierce, and as they reach the river another tree is struck by lightning. *This is getting seriously dangerous,* Thomasine thinks, and she decides to try and shelter under a patch of banana trees whose wide leaves afford some relief from the rain. Peering out through the banana fronds, Thomasine watches loose tree branches and debris propelled down the river whose water has turned brown from the mud washing into it.

Thomasine decides to stop trying to push forward until the storm abates a little. The patch of banana palms is a relative haven from the lightning, and she dismounts and coaxes Maisie to lie down on the ground. Sitting down and leaning back against Maisie's warm flank, Thomasine waits for some sign of a break in the storm. She also keeps a close eye out for snakes, but they seem to have gone to ground for the duration of the cloudbursts. The storm rages on for another hour and Thomasine begins to wonder if it will ever stop. Finally, it abates a little, although the rain remains heavy. It's now quite dark and she decides she and Maisie must battle on. Thoughts of *Ejuncum* leap into her mind. *We've got to get home, Maisie. We can't stay out in this bush all night.*

At very long last, Thomasine can see the lamps on the veranda at *Ejuncum*. Plodding up the track to the gate she sees Jack, and Edward, carrying a lantern, hurrying down the path towards her.

"Tommy, my darling! Thank God you're safe!" Jack cries out as he helps her down from the saddle. Edward leads Maisie off to be dried down and Jack hurries Thomasine inside.

"You have no idea how worried we've all been. I sent Edward and Roland off to look for you earlier, but they came back alone. I see now you sensibly chose to come back by the river. I'll boil up some hot water now and get you into a warm bath and then into bed. Are you alright? You haven't hurt yourself, have you?"

Thomasine sinks thankfully into her hot bath

"Never again will I venture out into a looming storm," she vows to Jack, who sits by her bathtub, holding her hand. "I'll stay overnight wherever I am in the future."

Jack tucks her up in bed with a cup of soup and some toast, and Thomasine is soon soundly asleep.

****

Having recovered from her journey through the storm in the bush, Thomasine then finds herself involved in a storm at home. She has been having more trouble with young Ina, now a very attractive – and flirtatious – 16 year old. All her life, Ina has played with the local boys, swimming in the creek, riding and sailing with them to school, and now starting to meet them at local dances.

"I need your advice, John," Thomasine says one evening as they sit at the dinner table with their visitor, John Brown, now a regular dinner guest. "I'm very worried and annoyed with Ina. She's now got herself engaged to six different boys – six! This can't go on, she'll get herself into real trouble soon – these country boys are grown men. This is not the way a nicely-brought-up girl should behave."

"Yes," John replies, "I've noticed myself how attractive she's becoming. She really should go to a school in Brisbane for a while and learn how to behave in polite society. She's bright and she could marry well if she were introduced to Brisbane society."

Thomasine and Jack nod in agreement. "We can't control her, I'm afraid," Thomasine admits. "John, do you think you could say something to her about these engagements? The matter is actually quite serious."

John, who is staying overnight at *Ejuncum*, agrees to have a word with Ina in the morning.

Next day, after breakfast, John takes Ina aside and invites her to go for a walk with him in the garden.

"Ina," he says, gently broaching the subject, "I hear you've gone and got yourself tangled up with six different young men. This must be a bit of a problem. How do you beat them off!"

Ina looks embarrassed and blushes. "Well," she admits, "I like them all – they've been my friends all my life. I couldn't say 'no' to them."

"I understand," John says. "You don't want to seem rude, but things have got a bit out of hand, haven't they? You're very young and you don't really want to get married for quite a while yet, do you? Wouldn't you like to get away from Nerang for a while and see the big wide world? And it's not really fair on these young men for you to have accepted all their proposals."

Ina, looking crestfallen, nods.

"I'll talk to your mother and we'll see what can be done to sort things out," John says.

Later, John and Thomasine sit out on the veranda and discuss what can be done.

"First of all," John suggests, "How about I help her write a little letter to each of the lads, explaining that she is honoured that he has proposed to her, but that she is soon to go to Brisbane to attend school and will be away for some time."

"What do you mean about her going away to Brisbane?" asks Thomasine in surprise.

"Well," John pauses, "Why don't you and Jack think about letting Ina come to live for a while in Brisbane with my sister, Louisa, and me? We could look after her safely and send her to an establishment there which teaches etiquette and dancing and so on, and introduce her gradually into Brisbane society. She's a lovely young girl and she'll be wasted on these farm boys. See if Jack agrees."

Thomasine and Jack discuss the idea and conclude that it is, indeed, a good plan. Ina is told about the idea, and she, too, thinks it's a sensible way of escaping the mix-up she has created.

So John sits her down with a pen and notepaper and helps her write to each of her six beaux. A month or so later, she sets off with Thomasine in a Cobb & Co coach with a suitcase of clothes which will soon be discarded for smarter town styles, and her new life begins.

Thomasine

****

Early in 1882, Jack decides to sell part of *Ejuncum*. The Cooper boys are grown up: Edward, Thomasine's second-eldest child, now 24, has in the previous March (1881) married his 17-year-old sweetheart, Lena Hayles, who had emigrated with her family to Nerang from Pontypool, Monmouthshire, in 1869. Roland is 22 and Herbert, "Bertie", is a strapping 19-year-old. May, (now 26 and mother of two), and her husband, Henry Schneider, have moved into their newly-built riverside house, and have begun their lifetime hobby of growing exotic and native plants in their greenhouse and garden. The younger Browne children, too, are growing up. Walter (Jack Jnr) is 16 and now very useful helping Jack. Faith, 14, and her sister, Ada, 12, are starting to blossom. This leaves only two youngsters: Lionel, aged 10 and Rosamond, nine, which means that both Jack and Thomasine can move on to new ventures.

Jack decides to sell the section of land he had bought after selling *Keith Farm* back in 1868 and where he had moved *Ejuncum* down from the hills. He sets about building a smaller *Ejuncum* back up the hill – a house more suited to their smaller family. Rather than putting the land down by the rive on the open market, Jack decides to sell it (or is it a wedding present?) to Edward, who happily settles there with Lena and their baby, Edo, the first of what will eventually be a family of ten children. Not long after Edward and Lena move in, Lionel and Bertie join them, and for a time, the three brothers are living in the one household.

Young Lena is a bright young woman, and because she is reasonably erudite, she has been a trainee teacher since the age of 13 and will eventually teach at a local school. Over the coming years she keeps a daily diary[2].

A typical entry jots down notes about the daily household activities:

"Monday March 22, 1867, Lucy washing. I made 6lbs guava jam
Weather – fine

Edward mended up the washing shed."

But her diary entries over the years also note down the comings-and-goings of family and friends as they plough their fields, cut their cane, or harvest their oats. The men often take their guns out into the countryside to shoot pigeon, ducks, partridges, and kangaroos. The extended family meets often for the church service at St Margaret's, and Lena reports that she undergoes Confirmation. Once a year there's the Duck Shoot at the Ejuncum Lagoon – a very special occasion. Lena rides her horse, Meteor, or takes the buggy to visit people or to shop at Nerang township where the stores stock an ever-wider range of goods. Despite the healthy outdoor life of Nerang, everyone suffers minor ailments and infectious diseases – like the mumps. By the time she has ten children, Lena finds coping with a measles outbreak very time-consuming as one family member after another comes out in spots. Lena describes how mustard plasters on the chest are the best remedy for colds and bronchitis, and mustard plasters on the head if someone falls over and hurts their head. Severe toothache is cured by a visit to the Southport dentist who either kills the nerve or pulls the tooth right out. Very occasionally, if someone is seriously ill, a telegram is sent to the local doctor to make a house call, or, if the patient is in dire straits, he or she is sent to the hospital at Southport.

Lena in 1880

Lena constantly sews new clothes and mends old ones for herself, Edward and Edo, and later on, her other children. She makes, and sells, butter and she boils up peach and apricot jam and bakes endless cakes which she serves up at family teas when her Haynes parents call in from Nerang township or the younger Brownes and other friends come down from *Ejuncum* for tea or to stay overnight. The Schneiders, May and Henry, also hold tea parties at their house farther along the riverbank, and sometimes Charles Philpott and his wife join in. Lena and Edward visit *Ejuncum* often, and Thomasine, and sometimes Jack, when he can be spared from his various duties, come to tea and dinner at Edward and Lena's, and Thomasine gives Lena regular piano lessons. When someone is ill in the household, Thomasine will often stay overnight to assist young Lena who has her hands full coping with her string of babies. She is causally matter-of-fact about their births and regularly notes, as she did on Friday 27th January 1893:

> "I taken ill about ½ past 4 AM. Got up at daylight & put things in their places, Edward got breakfast ready. Brought me a cup of tea before 7. Edward sent Charlie for Mrs Tuesley [nurse]. Baby born at 8.30 AM (a girl). Lionel came down for the buggy to take Miss Primrose to the station. Ada came in the afternoon. Edward went to Nerang for groats."

Young girls come and go as servants to help Lena with the washing and ironing and other household chores which include the occasional removal of a green or black snake which has found its way into the house or up into the roof. Snakes are a common hazard, as Lena writes in her diary on Monday 29th January 1883:

> "I cut out & sewed the seams of the dress mother gave.
> Baby sat up nearly all day. Edward saw a black snake eating a dead tiger snake.

Rolie went to post.
Weather very hot"

And on March 11th of that year she writes:

"Mrs Rogers came to wash – Louis Hanlon came just
after breakfast.
Rolie went to post. Mrs R took some citrons home
with her
Weather fine. Cold morning.
The boys killed a green snake in the house."

Another regular hazard for the denizens of Nerang is the recurring
floods. Sometimes the river fails to break its banks, but most years
it does. On January 22nd 1887, Lena recounts:

"Water all round. River & swamp met at the old
road out from the old place. Fred Sharp came up
with Mr Starkey's horses about eight o'clock. Lacy
took his horses up to Calaghan's paddock just
before that. Frank Parr went up with a boat to fetch
him back. Mr Starkey, Fred & Ned swam down to
the barn for flour – brought it back in the boat,
paddled the boat about among the orange trees &
over the corn in front of the house. Ned & Mr S went
down to the old place for pumpkins. Butc's came –
had to swim their horses in some places. Norman &
Tuesleys went down the road in a boat as far as
Kamholtz & brought his wife & children up to
Tuckers – water in their house up to their knees.
Kamholtz & the deaf & dumb brother would not
leave the place."

With no hairdresser or barber yet in Nerang, a lot of
haircutting and beard-trimming goes on in the household. At
Christmastime, Ina usually comes down from Brisbane for a
visit, staying at *Ejuncum* and riding around the district, visiting
family and friends before returning to Brisbane from Southport
on the steamer.

From time to time, Mr Taylor, the Inspector of Islanders, comes to check on Edward's Islander cane-cutting workforce

But it isn't all hard slog, there are concerts and dances and sometimes even a dance at *Ejuncum*. There are visits to town for lunch, and sometimes a wedding occurs. Lena gives an account of the Nerang fashions at a friend's wedding on November 15th 1887:

> "I got up & did the work & got the children ready to leave with their Grandmother Browne [Thomasine] while we went to Jessie & Maynard's wedding. Jessie wore white satin drapery of lace across the front. Black shoes. Teule (sic) veil orange wreath, bouquet of white gardenias & maidenhair. Lucy & Annie, white box dresses, wide blue ribbon, white sailor hats trimmed with blue. Molly & Gwennie white dresses trimmed with work. White sailor hats trimmed with blue. Mother, blue broche grenadine dress, grey bonnet with pink & grey feathers. Julia Hanlon, white box dress bag front wide pink satin sach (sic), white lace hat & parasol. Jessie's travelling dress, grey cashmere, grey velvet bonnet. I wore my wedding dress with white lace flounce in front net drapery at the back, cardinal belt & ribbons. Navy blue & cardinal bonnet. Rolie was best man. He, Mr Smales & Julia Hanlon the only guests invited out of the family. Mr & Mrs Maynard drove to Deep Water point at ½ past 2. Edward & I called at *Ejuncum* & then went down to Carara [*sic – should be Carrara*] with all the children had tea at Starkey's. Weather fine splendid day."

Edward, too, keeps a diary from year-to-year. He describes himself for the census as "gentleman farmer" but he is very much a hard-working, down-to-earth farmer, ploughing fields, pulling cattle and horses out of swamps, attending livestock sales, threshing and harvesting his crops – as his matter-of-fact diary entries like this one, reveal:

A Frightening Storm and a Stormy Daughter

"5 Tuesday, February 1878.
Went to Carara before breakfast.
Took the horses to water
Planting corn with boys & Papa
Went to post in the evening on Bronswing
Very cloudy all day rained a nice shower in the
 afternoon
Fine night after all
Butt came in the afternoon for flour."

Lena's constant references to *Ejuncum* in her diaries are to the latest incarnation of *Ejuncum*, erected in 1883 after Jack has decided to move the remainder of his household back up the hill to a new *Ejuncum*, built on the site of the original *Ejuncum*. He is now in his early 40s, and his various activities, now as Clerk of the Board, not Chairman, and his growing involvement in the agricultural association and the voluntary militia take up more of his time. As well, the Freemasons at Beenleigh and later, Southport, are to occupy him more. He also yearns for some mental stimulus, and to make some more money – he is finding mixed farming isn't particularly lucrative. First, he does some work as accountant at some sugar mills up the river, and at the *Gairlock Plantation* on the Herbert River, and in 1886 he takes over Mr Maynard's Auction Mart at Nerang. His earlier experience in the London auction house stands him in good stead, and this experience, coupled with his deep knowledge of the area and his gregarious nature, makes him highly successful.

END NOTES CHAPTER 20

[1] Family lore.

[2] Lena Browne's Diary, courtesy Sue Mills and the Local Studies Library, Southport.

21

Threats from Afar

WHILE NERANG and Southport are wrangling over monies spent on drains, a far bigger battle has been raging in South Africa between the British settlers and the Dutch; the First Boer War. It is also known as the First Anglo Boer War and the Transvaal War or Rebellion. It started on December 16th 1880 and the battles continued until March 23rd 1881.

Despite his being up to his ears in local politics with the birth of the Divisional Board, Jack's Indian Mutiny experience sets his nose twitching and he volunteers to fight the Boers – much to Thomasine's chagrin. But he is turned down for a good reason: he is now in his early forties and there are plenty of younger Australian men keen to fight – not that the British really need them.

Nevertheless, war fever ignites not only Jack, but many other Australians up and down the East Coast, and militias start to be set up, following the lead of Sydney, whose population has been protected more or less since the colony was founded.

It isn't just the Boer War that ignites this military fever in Australia. The earlier Crimean War of 1853-56 has already established a long-held fear of Russian invasion[1], coupled with the colonisation of the North Pacific by the Germans, the French, the Spanish and the Americans. Moreover, France has now annexed New Caledonia, closer to home. The people of NSW, now with stacks of gold bullion piled up in banks in Sydney after the Gold Rushes of the 1850s and 60s, feel vulnerable.

Queenslanders, too, feel vulnerable – after all, they are closer to any invading force coming down the Pacific. Their permanent army is virtually non-existent and thus, in 1878, in an effort to rectify this lack of manpower, Queensland passes the Volunteer Act. Within two years the Volunteer force has grown to 1,219 men. Drill halls are constructed, and volunteer posts established in potentially vulnerable areas, such as the mouths of rivers. For the Nerang-Southport area, a Volunteer post and drill hall is set up at South Passage, Southport, where sea and river traffic between Brisbane and Southport is regarded as needing protection. The passing of the Defence Act in 1884 and the repeal of the Volunteer Act sees the establishment of a permanent military force, and a militia is established with all males between certain ages liable to be conscripted if required. This militia is established in the metropolitan areas of the colony, while unpaid volunteer units continued in rural areas.

Jack in his Volunteers' uniform

Over the years ahead, particularly after 1885 when the threat of a Russian invasion increases, Jack throws himself into this Volunteer military activity, gradually moving up the ranks from lieutenant to captain. As an outstanding horseman, he is a leader in the formation of the Southport mounted rifle corps.

The *Queenslander's*[2] correspondent reports on the meeting in the Southport School of Arts to form the rifle corps: "A numerous and enthusiastic muster of the manhood of Southport responded to the invitation, men in the prime of life forming the majority of the assembly". The paper reports its leaders vowing: "We are quite able to meet the Russians and demolish them or any other aggressors."

In the event, no foreign power ever invades Australia until the Second World War when the Japanese bomb Darwin and also send submarines down the East Coast. Nevertheless, over the coming years, Jack and his mates enjoy their military camaraderie and their mess dinners. His outgoing personality fits him well for the activities of the voluntary militia.

END NOTES CHAPTER 21

[1] *Australian War Scares of the Nineteenth Century*, Paper delivered in 1968 by Clem Lack, University of Queensland Library.

[2] *The Queenslander* July 9th 1885.

22

Nerang Grows Up

Thomasine, (standing centre), with Jack (far left) and three of her daughters (unidentified) and Lionel (right), plus favourite dogs

EVER SINCE JACK and Thomasine built their first *Ejuncum*, and later moved it down closer to the river, they have held musical evenings and dances there, but by 1884 the people of Nerang are also enjoying concerts, magic lantern shows, public meetings and other events at a small music hall built by Cockerill of the Royal Mail Hotel. The hall is built on land that will later be known as Bischoff Park. Cockerill names it Tobin's Music Hall, after his licensee, Stephen Tobin.

Such activity heralds the next stage of Nerang's growth: the establishment of a Nerang School of Arts.

In 1884, Thomasine and Jack, Edward and William Philpott (who has married Stephen Tobin's daughter, Nellie Veronica), hold a fund-raising concert at Tobin's Music Hall in aid of the Nerang Cricket Club. The concert's success leads to further fund-raising events for various deserving causes until the little music hall is destroyed in a cyclone.

After the music hall is blown down and washed away in the flood, Thomasine declares: "We must set up a proper School of Arts for Nerang, Southport has one already – and I've heard they only have a population of about 1000!" And this time, we'll make sure the hall is built away from the flood area – and large enough for a proper dance floor, a stage, a library and catering facilities."

The School of Arts project is close to completion in June 1887 when the township of Nerang celebrates Queen Victoria's Jubilee with fireworks, a 16-foot-high bonfire with an entire bullock turning on a spit, and balloons sent high above the town.

"If we had our School of Arts, we could have held a celebratory concert," Thomasine says with regret. "Still, we'll have it built by next year."

A series of fund-raising efforts produces sufficient funds, and in 1888 the Nerang School of Arts and Mechanics' Institute, standing on the corner of Ferry and Cotton Streets, is opened by E.J.Stevens, MLA, with a fanfare of activities including a bazaar, maypole dancing and a concert. Many locals have donated books, some of them quite precious heirlooms brought out from "Home", and when the building is opened the Institute's library boast 400 publications on its shelves. Daily and weekly newspapers and periodicals are also available in the library's reading room. [1]

Thomasine has taken out her old sewing machine – the wedding present of Uncle Keith – and this time creates something more useful and important than the red flannel shirts she ran up for her ungrateful Aboriginal kitchen staff back in 1873. This time she makes an enormous Union Jack to fly on the building's flagpole and she is elected a Life Member of the Institute in honour of her involvement in raising the funds to build it. She continues to be a leading light at the concerts where her singing voice is applauded.

With the School of Arts completed, the following year the newly built Queen's Hotel opens its doors near the soon-to-be-ready railway station, bringing Nerang's hotel quota to four. A steel girder railway bridge is being erected over the river.

Indeed, with tourism booming in Southport and the timber industry pushed to keep up with demand from new housing developments, the entire South Queensland area is prospering.

With her family now almost all grown up, Thomasine has more time to devote to her musical and other activities. Edward is now 30, and Lena is 23 and well on her way to having a family of ten children. Roland is 29 and Herbert (Bertie) is 26, and they have been also living and working at *Birribon*. Ina is now 24. Walter John is 23, Faith, 21, Ada, 19, Lionel, 13, and Rosamond, 12.

****

Like Thomasine and Jack's children, Nerang is growing up in the 1880s, and with the arrival of the railway in 1889, Nerang can be said to have come of age. Thomasine, Jack, and family join the rest of Nerang on July 15th at the little timber railway station, sited in the aptly-named Station Street on the south side of the river, close to where the Browne family had moved their encampment up the hill from the flooding river back in 1867. The Nerang railway station[2] is the final stop of the South Coast line from Brisbane to Beenleigh which was opened in 1885. Later, in 1902, the line will extend to Tweed Heads and Southport.[3]

Nerang railway station

Thomasine

As the Station Master flags down the first steam engine to arrive at the station on that historic day in 1889, the town of Nerang, although 49 miles 11 chains (78.6km) south of Brisbane, suddenly becomes part of the modern late Victorian world. Travel between Nerang and Brisbane is no longer by slow coach along muddy, often swampy, roads, and the timber and agricultural products can be carried to Brisbane by rail instead of by ship. Commerce prospers from the day the little railway station opens and the people of Nerang congratulate themselves for living in a town which now has a working telephone system, delivery of the Brisbane newspapers daily by rail, and local shops stocked with a wide variety of food and clothing.

Thomasine and Jack too, having sold part of *Ejuncum*, and with Jack's purchase of the auction house, are now able to sit back a little and enjoy the fruit of their labours. With grandchildren arriving they are starting to be called "Grandma and Grandpa". Jack's decision to give up part of *Ejuncum* and to turn to other forms of employment are to prove wise moves. But as yet, optimism prevails at Nerang and there's no portent of the dark days to come.

END NOTES CHAPTER 22

[1] The School of Arts was moved from Ferry and Cottons Streets in 1929 to Price Street on land donated by William Henry Spencer. It was re-named the Nerang Community Hall in the 1980s or possibly later.

[2] The station building has been moved several times over the years, but its final resting place is at the Gold Coast Hinterland Heritage Museum at Mudgeeraba.

[3] The Nerang-Tweed Heads extension was closed in 1961. Nerang once again became the terminus, until the entire line was closed in 1964, replaced by the Pacific Motorway.

23

Ina

Ina, aged about 20

BY 1893, Thomasine and Jack's eldest daughter, Ina, has been a resident of Brisbane for 12 years, and much has happened in that time. After attending Mrs Green's small, exclusive, school where she is taught how to dance and learn items of etiquette to help her behave politely in Brisbane society, she is launched by Louisa Brown into the round of dances and balls and other social activities of the wealthy members of Brisbane society, With her dainty figure, long red hair and winsome manner she is soon feted as the "belle of the ball". The local young men gather around her, and Ina, as is her want, flirts merrily with them. Proposals of marriage start to arrive, but she turns them down – she is enjoying being in the spotlight and she likes this male attention. Lena Cooper's diary in 1883 mentions in passing that Ina, now 18, has got engaged, but this seems to have been a short-lived arrangement. However, perhaps a broken heart changes her attitude, for after two years or so, by which time she is 21, Ina starts to tire of the Brisbane social scene and has turned to religion. Her old friends, irked by her sudden conversion, complain that she accosts them with religious tracts. This, however, is a passing phase, but nevertheless, the old, devil-may-care Ina is calming down.

Walking out onto the veranda one hot afternoon at John Brown and his sister Louisa's home, *Helenleigh*, in Norfolk Road, South Brisbane, Ina finds John sitting sipping ale and reading Goethe. Hesitantly, she confides to him: "You know, John, these young men are so shallow! I'm used to good country boys who know how to deliver a calf or plough a field or sail a boat. These city boys can barely open a door properly.

"I think I shan't attend so many of these parties any longer. I prefer to stay at home with you and Louisa and listen to your stories about when you were a surveyor and went out into the dense bush and up unexplored rivers and I like to hear what you've been doing all day in your important job with the Government."

And so Ina becomes closer to John Brown until they mutually agree they enjoy one another's company and they decide to marry. "Now I'll be Thomasina Brown without the 'e'!" Ina laughs. The wedding takes place in Brisbane on August 30th 1887. with Thomasine and Jack thankful that Ina has settled down at last. She is now 22 and John 57 – a very wide age gap – but Ina doesn't care.

"I shall be happy with you, John Brown," she declares. [1]

They soon have a daughter, Clara,[2] and just under four years later, a son, John. Ina, and sometimes John snr., visit *Ejuncum* and Nerang, usually at Christmas, and Ina spends up to a month there, riding around the countryside visiting old friends.

Ina

Ina and Clare

In 1893, Brisbane, in particular, is hit badly by the unusually big floods of that year. Ina, now 29 and still living at *Helenleigh* in Norfolk Road, looks out of her window and witnesses, at first-hand, the devastation caused by the rising waters of the Brisbane River. She sees entire warehouses and wharves washed away and she learns that many houses in low-lying areas have been destroyed. Although the Brown residence is sited on sufficiently high ground to avoid the floodwaters, several cottages John Brown owns in low-lying parts of town are washed away.

"We should go out and see what we can salvage from our cottages," John suggests, and he and Ina don mackintoshes and rubber boots and wade out into the flood to rescue doors and windows from John's residential investments floating by.

John is not only a victim of the floods, he has also been a victim of the financial downturn that Queensland and the rest of Australia are beginning to experience. He is retrenched by the now-bankrupt government, along with many other civil servants, He is rescued by a friend who employs him as a clerk in his office until John can eventually return to his civil service career where he is to rise to become Deputy Registrar General of Queensland.

END NOTES CHAPTER 23

[1] And indeed, she was. After John died from pneumonia, in 1916 Ina never married again, remaining faithful to her "dear John". Ref: Barbara Jobson *Memoirs*.

[2] My grandmother, Clara Maude Adah, later re-named Clare, married Paul Jenner Ure on March 28th 1910.

24

From Boom to Bust – The 1890s

THE EUPHORIA THOMASINE and Jack and the other residents of Nerang experienced with the arrival of the railway in Nerang has been short-lived. As early as 1890 signs of a weakening in the Queensland economy begin to emerge. The timber industry starts to receive dwindling orders because fewer houses and buildings are going up, and the sugar industry also begins to feel the pinch. In August of that year the Herman Musical Troupe plays to poor houses, and, to Thomasine's dismay, the Nerang School of Arts' annual income suddenly drops from £59/6/7 in 1888-89 to only £7/3/4 in 1889-90.[1]

More seriously, a growing number of farmers begin to face bankruptcy. Fortunately, Jack has predicted the bad times looming and has sold off parts of *Ejuncum*, so the family manages to keep on farming and selling their butter and other products, but, to augment their finances Jack is now busily involving himself in other income-producing activities which will stand him and Thomasine and the family in good stead in the difficult years to come.

But others are not so prescient, and many are suffering both drought and then floods, their crops are ruined, and they can't pay their mortgages. They and their families are left with nothing. Some of the owners of larger properties, like David Fullarton of *Bundall*, are also facing financial problems. This is the large plantation close to the mouth of the river which Thomasine and Jack had gazed at from their cutter back in 1864, when it was the only cultivated property on the Nerang. Now insolvent, Fullarton is forced to sell the last vestiges of the once great plantation.

Jack finds himself selling off more and more bankrupt farms at his auction business, a task he doesn't relish.

Sawmills start to close, and in 1893 all banks south of Beenleigh are shut down. In Nerang, although its four pubs manage to survive, the town is to be left with no bank until 1905 after the closure of the Bank of NSW.

These dire signs of a financial crisis in Southern Queensland mirror a far deeper monetary crisis elsewhere in Australia, and soon the rest of the world, culminating in the Great Depression of 1892-93. The uncontrolled property boom of the 1880s, fired by a rapid growth in bank and building society lending, coupled with uncontrolled banking activity and some times fraud, are at the root of the crisis.[2]

****

The severe floods of 1893, which Ina and John Brown personally experience, prolong the financial crisis in Southern Queensland where widespread devastation of corn stored in flooded barns and other crops in flooded fields force even more farmers off their land.

The floods of 1893, severe as they are, do, however, stimulate a move by a group of landowners to get the sugar cane business up and running again. Among this group of land-owners is Thomasine's eldest son, Edward, who is soon to follow in Jack's footsteps and become a member of the Nerang Divisional Board, along with Jack, who is still Board Clerk despite being forced by the financial crisis to drop his annual salary by £15.[3] Because so many landowners cannot manage to pay their rates any longer, the Divisional Board has sacked all its maintenance staff, and thus roads and bridges suffer neglect – the roads, particularly after the floods, becoming impassable in some areas.

The landowners, working together to revive the ailing sugar industry, form a consortium to take advantage of the Sugar Works Guarantee Act of 1893 and start the Nerang River Sugar Company and begin growing cane at Carrara, and the now sub-divided estates of *Bundall* and *Benowa*. In 1895 the Nerang Divisional Board, which has been meeting in a barn all these years, moves to a purpose-built building at Mudgeeraba. By 1896 a new, state of the art sugar mill is crushing cane, hampered in its first year of operation by the worst frosts the area has ever suffered in the locals' experience. Edward, like many other farmers, hedges his bets by also moving into pig farming and dairying. His and Lena's diaries tell of extra cows being bought and butter being churned daily (mainly by Lena) to sell into the market.

By 1900, Nerang's future, and that of the rest of south-east Queensland, has stabilised. Sugar cane, timber, dairying and pig farming are all prospering, while the emerging tourist trade at Southport and the developing area which will become the Gold Coast are starting to transform the entire coastal area.

As she digs in her garden at *Ejuncum* and looks down at the newly-planted fields below her, Thomasine, the Browne family matriarch, thanks God, thinking *Well, the Browne family has managed to survive the bad times. All looks bright – except I'm worried about Jack's health. He's not at all his usual hearty self.*

END NOTES CHAPTER 24

[1] *Nerang Shire, op cit.*, p122.

[2] "Counting banks as any institution that called itself a bank and solicited public deposits, 54 of the 64 institutions operating in 1891 had closed by mid-1893; 34 of these closed permanently. Defining banks more narrowly, to exclude institutions more akin to building societies, only nine of 28 banks remained open continuously throughout the 1890s. Of the banks that suspended payment, six closed permanently (either failing outright or being taken over). Several of the banks that reopened were later taken over by stronger banks. At the height of the crisis in April and May 1893, the banks that suspended payment accounted for 56 per cent of deposits and 61 per cent of the note issue in the six Australian colonies." Ref: Reserve Bank of Australia RDP 2001-07: *A History of Last-Resort Lending and Other Support for Troubled Financial Institutions in Australia.*

[3] Longhurst, Robert, *Nerang Shire, op cit.*

25

A Brave Beginning and a
Sad End

EARLY ON THE morning of January 1ˢᵗ 1901, Thomasine is out in her vegetable garden, picking tomatoes and digging up lettuces for a big *Ejuncum* lunch to celebrate the new unification of the Australian States, which has been building up over the previous year with conferences and a series of referenda. Finally all the States[1] agree, and the deed is done; the Commonwealth of Australia is declared.

Do I feel I'm an Australian? Thomasine ponders. *Well yes, and no. I certainly still feel English – but I wouldn't want to be living back there. Nonetheless, I'm very proud of my British heritage and all that we stand for.*

Perhaps, if anything, I might regard myself as a Queenslander. Certainly, I love this country we have made our home in. But it will probably take the children, and their children, to really feel Australian through and through.

Nerang, like every country town and rural community, stages its own Federation celebrations with streets decorated with flags, and bonfires and fireworks lighting up the evening. Nerang school puts on a celebratory display and the pupils write poems and sing songs commemorating the event. The Nerang shops are aflutter with souvenir handkerchiefs, and teapots, vases, mugs and plates sport celebratory designs. The town's pubs do a hearty trade, and the local farmers, like Thomasine and Jack, invite their families and friends to celebratory lunches.

At the lunch table that memorable day, Thomasine asks her family and guests how they feel about Australia. "I definitely feel part of Nerang and Queensland," Edward declares, "and yes, I guess I belong here. I really don't remember much of England now."

May echoes him. "Henry and I feel Australian," she says. "We go out into the bush and find marvellous Australian plants for our wildflower collection. They're not like English flowers – their colours are beautiful but not pretty – and they're somehow tougher – able to withstand the heat and the heavy rain. English flowers would wilt here."

Jack thinks for a moment. "Even as a child," he says, "I yearned for distant horizons. I had thought of living in India, but Australia has been the right choice. What I particularly like about this country is its newness. In England everyone behaves the way their forefathers behaved. And I like the way the English class system has broken down here. I've met and befriended people from all walks of life and I enjoy their company.

"And now," Jack adds, raising his glass, "Let us toast our dear Queen Victoria, who is presently very ill. God bless our Queen – the Queen of England and Australia!" They all raise their glasses to the Monarch.

Ina, who is making her regular Christmas-New Year visit to Nerang, has the last word: "Even though I was born in a tent – people still make fun of me for that – I wouldn't want to live anywhere else. Anyway, England's so far away, I can't really even imagine it."

Three weeks after the diners at the Nerang table have toasted Queen Victoria, the Queen dies, aged 81.

Lena Cooper notes this event in her diary:

22 TUESDAY
The Queen died. The whole world in deep sorrow.

For Jack, the Queen's death means a change of plan for his much-awaited presentation as a member of the Southport Volunteers to Prince Edward. This was to have taken place in Brisbane in late May 1901. However, Prince Edward, now King, must remain in London to prepare for the late Queen's funeral, and thus his son Prince George, who had previously visited Queensland as a 16 year old midshipman, returns as the Duke of Cornwall and York, with his wife, Mary (they later become King George V and Queen Mary).[2]

Watching Jack looking splendid in his full scarlet dress uniform and saluting the Duke at the presentation, Thomasine is both proud and worried. *He's so handsome and carries himself so well,* she muses, *and he's been so successful both as a farmer and in his work for Nerang, but I'm still worried about his health.* She is concerned that he has been suffering bladder and kidney problems for several months and is in severe pain from time to time.

I can see the effects of his illness in his face, Thomasine thinks as she watches Jack chatting with the Duke. *But he won't slow down and relax – he works too hard for everybody.*

*Jack in full-dress uniform at his
presentation to the Duke of Cornwall*

On their return to Nerang from Brisbane, Jack starts telling people he doesn't think he has much time left on Earth. He mentions the recent deaths of two of his brothers: Charles, in 1891 at the age of 50, and Edmond, also 50, the following year, followed by the death of his sister, Harriet, at 58, in 1899. His condition worsens after the trip to Brisbane, and he is forced to take to his bed. The doctor visits, but nothing he prescribes manages to alleviate the pain. However, on August 11th, Jack gets up and declares he's now fit enough to ride down to

Southport that evening for a drill and mess dinner with his Volunteer regiment.

"I miss my mates," he tells Thomasine. "I'm feeling much better, and a bit of a ride will do me the world of good."

Thomasine attempts to dissuade him, but, knowing Jack, she realises that once he's made up his mind to do something, nothing and nobody can stop him.

He sets off for Southport in the late afternoon, kissing Thomasine goodbye as he walks out the door of *Ejuncum*.

"Goodbye, Tommy, I'll probably be back quite early," he promises.

"Take care, Jack," is all Thomasine can say.

"I'll see you later tonight," Jack replies, "or, if I'm late, I'll sleep in the other bedroom tonight so as not to wake you."

When Jack doesn't return early that night. Thomasine isn't particularly worried. He often stays overnight with friends in Southport, particularly if the mess dinner has been an especially convivial one.

But early next morning, there is still no sign of him. Lionel then goes outside and finds his father's horse at the gate with the bridle dangling. He calls to his sister, Faith, to go and see if their father is in the bed he sometimes uses when returning home late at night. Not finding him there and noticing the bed hasn't been slept in, she rushes to Thomasine's bedroom and wakens her and then back to Lionel and sends him off to search for Jack. Lionel gallops off, looking everywhere for his father. Then, when he reaches the foot of the hill at the racecourse, he discovers his father lying face upward, dead, in the shallow water table. Lionel doesn't stop to look further and goes straight on to the police who hurry to the water table with some of the townspeople who help Lionel carry Jack's body back to *Ejuncum*.[3]

Thomasine is shocked to the core. How could Jack have fallen off his horse? She knows he's one of the best horsemen in Queensland. What could have happened?

Lena recounts in her diary: on Tuesday 13th August:

"Willie came down first thing in the morning to say that Granpa Browne was dead. Edward & I went to *Ejuncum* at once. Lionel when he got up at daylight saw his father's horse at the gate with the bridle dangling...They had just got him washed & laid out when I reached *Ejuncum*...people came from Tallebudgera. Rolie Jack & Annie, Ina & her children came from Brisbane. Letters & telegrams from lots...It is a fearful blow for the whole family. Lionel, Faith & their mother are bearing up splendidly & cheering the rest. Rolie, Jack & Lionel walked down with me after tea. May, Ada & Geoff & Julia came during the day."

Thomasine is numb with the shock of losing her dear Jack. At first, though, she thinks about the other members of the family, some of whom are distraught at the death of their much-loved father and grandfather, and the little ones are bewildered and frightened and need comforting. Thomasine rallies to pull the assembled family together: she has always been strong. Her grief will come later

In the report of his death in the *Brisbane Courier*, Wednesday August 14th 1901, it states:

"[Captain Browne...] was found drowned[4] in a waterhole this morning...between Southport and Nerang. He was at Southport at last night's drill, and left for home about 8.30 o'clock, riding a spirited horse. It is supposed that he was thrown. The horse was found near the fence early this morning. The deceased was highly popular and respected throughout the district. He was always foremost in any movement conducive to progress or sports and was clerk of the Nerang Board and Secretary to the Agricultural Society. The unfortunate gentleman leaves a widow and a grown-up family to mourn their loss. There will be a military funeral at Nerang at 3 o'clock tomorrow afternoon."

A full military funeral for Jack is held on Thursday August 15th at 3pm at the Nerang Anglican church – the biggest funeral Nerang has ever witnessed. Virtually everyone in the area comes to it. A procession of sulkies, carts and wagons and even a couple of carriages queues along the roadway into Nerang for half-a-mile.

The *Brisbane Courier* reported:

> "Preceding the hearse the members of G Company and Southport Rifle Club marched with Rev H H Dixon on horseback. Lieutenants G Lather, R Johnson, Walsh and Maddock were pall bearers, then came Majors Selheim and W Lather. Deceased's sons and relatives were next followed by members of Nerang Divisional Board and Agricultural Society, walking. Forty-three vehicles and 100 horsemen made up the remainder of the procession which was close on three quarters of a mile long!"

The report goes on to say that the Anglican Church bells tolled and business in Nerang came to a standstill. The report also stated that Captain Browne was buried in his scarlet uniform. Excerpts from a long obituary in *The Queenslander* on Saturday August 31st 1901, read:

> "...We began to think of the thousand good things we could say of him. Our thoughts ran back to times of accident, and whose help came first; of sudden demands for the doctor, and whose horse would go fastest...
>
> Mrs. Browne and all her children...may rest assured that, a great heartthrob of genuine regret has pulsed from end to end of the district. If we could only speak with the dead, we might find voice to say, "You have answered the 'Last post' with your trapping on: May God give you rest."

Thomasine sums up the sad event in a letter to William:

> *"It was very sudden at last, for after being ill for a week in bed most of that time, he rallied and went about his public work as usual and*

worked up to the last and as the paper infers died in harness.

It was a terrible shock to all of his family and to me you may be sure after living together for nearly 37 years. 'Through sunshine and shower'. For some years he had been suffering from a complaint of the bladder and kidneys and at times was in great agony so that his death is a merciful relief from his earthly sufferings and I think he must have been prepared in his own mind as he told us repeatedly that he did not expect to last long and said the same to no end of people besides. The thing we feel most acutely is that his horse threw him into some shallow water in a water table not far from home and he was not drowned so it must have been a sudden pang of the heart and the doctor says he most likely was dead before he fell.

There was no scratch or bruise or disfigurement and when he was laid out he looked like a beautiful wax model. He was one of the handsomest most aristocratic *looking men that Queensland ever saw."*

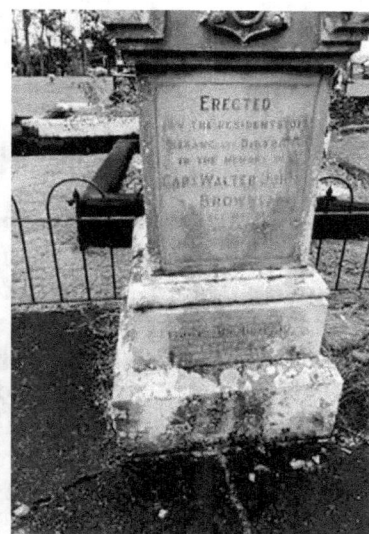

*Jack's grave and memorial plinth in Nerang Cemetery. Thomasine
is subsequently buried here too.*

Jack's pioneering contribution to the growth and
development of the Nerang district is commemorated today
by a bridge spanning the Pacific Motorway leading into
Nerang, which is named the ***Walter J Browne Bridge***

END NOTES CHAPTER 25

[1] Western Australia later contemplated seceding, but this did not occur.

[2] The first royal visitor to Queensland was Prince Alfred, the second son of
Queen Victoria (later to become the Duke of Edinburgh). A Royal Navy
Captain on a world tour on board HMS *Galatea* he visited Queensland in
March 1868. The second royal visit to Australia was when the Princes Edward
and George visited from 16th to 20th August 1881, while serving as
midshipmen on HMS *Bacchante*.

[3] Reported in the *Brisbane Courier* Wednesday 14th Aug 1901,
  Actually, he was not found drowned. He had apparently died while still on
horseback and had then fallen into the water table.

26

Aftermath

THOMASINE IS PRIVATELY devastated at the loss of Jack. Her mind turns over so many memories: Jack bearing the news of her father's murder; Jack taking her and the children to the Crystal Palace; the voyage to Australia; life in a tent; Jack delivering Ina; their happy times at *Ejuncum*. She stops and turns her mind to everyday matters, taking up her piano teaching, singing at concerts at the School of Arts, and looking after her grandchildren. Above all, she is, after all, the Browne family Matriarch, and without Jack, it is her role to be head of the family and keep the show on the road.

"I must get on with things," she tells May one morning over a cup of tea. "I suppose that's what I've done all my life." Her religious faith bolsters her too.

She writes to William:

"We are all bending to our burden of grief in a resigned spirit for we feel that our loss is the dear departed's gain and we trust he rests in peace with Jesus and hope to meet him again in Heaven, . And I know I shall meet Jack again in Heaven – where I hope he is now well and happy." [1]

For many years, she continues to ride through the bush to outlying properties to teach the children there how to play the piano. When Ina brings Clare and John to stay, Thomasine teaches Clare how to play sophisticated melodies by Brahms and other composers, and she brings the family together for regular dances and lunches at *Ejuncum*.

Despite her protestations that all her life she has suffered from a heart complaint, Thomasine shows no sign of letting up from her energetic activities – even when she reaches the age of 82, she's still able to alight from a sulky unaided. She takes particular pride in the Agricultural Society and as late as the last show she takes part in, she is a winner for sauces, wines and needlework.

Octavia Cooper's *Memoirs* p 20 describe Thomasine in her 80s as a brilliant pianist who also has a sweet singing voice, singing such melodies at concerts as *Cherry Ripe and The Brook*.

In early 1916, when Thomasine is now 83, she feels it's time to leave *Ejuncum:*

> "I have left my home at Ejuncum, the other side of the Nerang River and come to live just opposite with my eldest daughter, May [at Umpinnido]," she writes in March 1916.

Two months after this letter is written, Thomasine dies after an attack of bronchitis and pneumonia at *Umpinnido* on May 15th 1916.

Her obituary in the *Queenslander*[2] gives a concise and reasonably accurate summary of her life and then comments:

> "The deceased lady always took a great interest in everything for the benefit of the district. She was for many years a Sunday School teacher and organist at St Margaret's Church of England and through her efforts the first organ for the church was bought. The Nerang School of Arts of which institution she was elected a life member had its beginnings in a glee club formed in her house and consisting largely of members of her family. She took particular pride in the

Agricultural Society so late as the last show a prize winner for sauces wines and needlework. …Many of the old hands will well remember the ever ready cup of tea at the old house and Mrs Browne's solicitude for the comfort and welfare of them and their friends."

This polite, very prim tribute barely touches on the real Thomasine: the woman who threw away a comfortable, privileged, life in London to sail up the Nerang to a new world.

It is difficult to know exactly what Thomasine's Will contained. Appended to her genealogy (written around 1901-3) she lists her investments: "My income is invested in the name of Mary Catherine Cooper, my trustee in Two and three quarter percent Consoles   one thousand two hundred and thirty seven pounds nine shillings and four pence.

Three and a half percent India stock = one hundred pounds.

One share in South Australia Co of twenty pounds share.

Excess of Income Tax is applied for the year ending April 3rd 1896.

Dividends applied (once taxed) for April 1897 and April 1898 two pounds four shillings and up to April 5, 1903."

There were also some jewels which Thomasine left to her Cooper children because they had originally belonged to her first husband, the Rev Edward James Cooper's father, the Rev. James Cooper[3]

Octavia Cooper's memoirs pp16-17 report "Grandma Browne had a wonderful lot of diamonds which she gave to the eldest children of her four Cooper children. Dad's eldest sister (his only one) had a son, viz Hal Carlton who gave his wife a large single diamond ring which belonged to the Rev Edward Cooper who was educated at Oxford University and Grandma Browne gave my eldest brother Edward a seven stone ring of white Indian diamonds!"

Octavia, known as Tave, went on to say "Grandma Browne (my father's mother) who married Captain Walter John Browne had a marriage settlement from her first husband, my father's father, and they took eight hundred pounds from it to pay their passages to Australia in the *Queen of the Colonies* in 1864. No more of this money was spent until the three Cooper brothers and Auntie May Carlton and their spouses had passed away and so my mother was entitled to it. She divided it with her 4 daughters (with accrued interest) after all those years. The Coopers also left money in Chancery which took a lawsuit lasting four years before my eldest brother got a slice of the cake together with the eldest of my father's cousins' families. After my brother passed away his son Eddo (my nephew) got the remaining crumbs."

Lena Cooper writes:

"Captain and Mrs Browne were energetic workers for every good cause and institution whether school, church (no matter what creed) or sport."

Thomasine is buried next to Jack in the cemetery at Nerang, beneath a large monument over the grave in the form of an obelisk with a sword engraved on it, which was erected by subscriptions from the citizens of Nerang.

Today most of the descendants of the Brownes and Coopers are scattered far and wide with few affiliations with Nerang. *Birribon*, which stood for over 100 years, was pulled down, and the land is now part of the Carrara Sports Complex. *Ejuncum* is now the Allambe Garden of Memories, and for many years a jacaranda and a palm tree existed on the site to indicate where the house once stood.[4]

Thomasine's indomitable courage and enthusiasm for life has been an inspiration to her descendants. She and her equally-courageous and enthusiastic husband, Jack, were pioneers in the true sense of the word, creating and building a new world for themselves and their descendants.

As Lena Cooper reminisced: "They were never wealthy in worldly goods but they possessed more wealth in the affection of their neighbours."

END NOTES CHAPTER 26

[1]Thomasine to her brother, William, no date, but shortly after Jack's death.

[2] *The Queenslander*, June 17th 1916, p.16.

[3] Sue Mills, a descendant of Thomasine and her first husband, the Rev. Edward James Cooper, provided this information about the diamonds: In the will of (Samuel) Edward Cherrill who was the father in law of Rev James Cooper he leaves the following

"and I give to my daughter Amelia the wife of the Reverend James Cooper one of my diamond rings and I direct that both of my said three children Alfred Nelson, Caroline Matilda and Amelia according to seniority of birth shall as soon as conveniently may be after my decease make choice of one of my diamond rings in satisfaction of the bequest ..."

"I give unto my said son in law James Cooper all the rest of my snuff boxes not herein before specifically bequeathed and also one pair of gold sleeve buttons"

In the will of Phiiladelphia Cherrill – wife of the above mentioned (Samuel) Edward Cherrill

"I hereby give and bequeath the said sum of One thousand one hundred pounds subject only to the payment of my debts funeral and testamentary expenses to my six children viz. Caroline Matilda Pizey widow Amelia Cooper (the wife of the Reverend James Cooper) Sidney Cherrill Adolphus Cherrill Montague Cherrill and Alfred Nelson Cherrill to be divided equally between them ..."

"The rest of my jewellery not herein before specifically bequeathed and my wearing apparel I give to my two daughters Caroline Matilda Pizey and Amelia Cooper to be equally divided between them"

[4] *Two Families, op cit.*, p20.

APPENDIX A

A Very Brief Outline of Early New Zealand History

THE TWO ISLANDS of New Zealand were first colonised at least 800 years ago by Polynesians down from the Pacific islands to the north, who established a strong tribal presence based on a system of kinship and land ownership.

The British were not the first Europeans to come to New Zealand – it had first been visited by a Dutchman, Abel Tasman, in 1642, followed in 1769 by Englishman James Cook and later by a motley collection of American and European whalers, escaped convicts of various nationalities, explorers, Christian missionaries, and adventurers – all hoping to find treasure of one sort or another.

But it was the British who had seriously and systematically settled there in the 19th Century. Gradually more and more British settlers arrived, accompanied by the British Army, and later, some Australian troops, sent by the British Government, whose intention was to colonise the country for Britain and make it part of the British Empire.

The result was a land with two almost separate cultures; the British and the Maori – and they behaved almost independently – as if the newcomers didn't exist to the Maori, and vice versa to the British – except for some trading between them. Very few Maoris entered the homes of the English settlers, nor did many English ever enter a Maori dwelling, The Maoris spoke their own language but many of them also spoke English quite well – and some of them were Christians, converted by the early missionaries. They had their own weapons – clubs and spears – but they also used the English weapons.

If the British Government hadn't been hellbent on turning them into British citizens, the Maoris and the 'outsettlers' might have managed to live together amicably. (After all, it *had been* the Maoris' country all that long time.)

The British governors were backed up by a massive military presence. By the mid-19th century the number of British troops stationed there approached 18,000, compared to the 4,000 Maori warriors. The number of British settlers at that time was about 1,000.

The bilingual Treaty of Waitangi was the first formal attempt to come to grips with the relationship between the British and the Maoris.[1] However, the Treaty mandated that Queen Victoria's government gained the sole right to purchase Maori land.[2]

The 1840s saw many inter-tribal battles, sometimes called the "Musket Wars".

Gradually some Maori tribes had begun to disintegrate due to the influence of alcohol and other European practices such as prostitution.

Since 1856 race relations had become a major problem. Responsible government had been introduced then, but the Governor decided to keep native affairs under his personal control.

All the while the South Island, which had much more pastoral grazing land, saw little or no fighting. However, land was not the No. 1 reason for the conflict. Sovereignty over the Maoris by the British was probably the root cause.

The consequences of this led to what were called the Maori Wars, or the Land Wars – now called the New Zealand Wars – and the conflict continued until 1872. Race relations were exacerbated by the increasing pressure by the colonists who wanted more of the Maori land. Many Maori tribes joined the Kingitanga (Maori King) movement, placing their land under the protection of a single figure – a Maori king.[3]

During the Merediths' first year in New Zealand the First Taranaki War (March 17th 1860 to March 18th 1861) broke out in the Taranaki area to the south-west of Auckland, over land ownership and the imposition of British sovereignty on the Maori population. The war was to continue for a year there, involving more than 3,500 imperial troops brought in from Australia, plus volunteers from the local community, versus around 1,500 Maori men, women and children. The war ended in a ceasefire, with neither side admitting defeat. An uneasy truce was negotiated, but Governor Thomas Gore Browne was determined to completely defeat the Maori King movement and planned to reignite hostilities. Browne was then dismissed and was replaced by Governor Sir George Grey in September 1861. Grey, who had quite some rapport with the Maoris and had even learned their language, suspended Browne's plans for invasion of the Maori-held territory. For the next 18 months it looked as if further war had been averted.

But then, in March 1863, Grey went to Taranaki and re-occupied the Maori territory there. A series of relatively minor battles ensued, and a number of Maoris and British troops were killed. After that, Taranaki was deemed to have quietened-down and most of the British troops were moved to Auckland and the Waikato area to its south. Next, on July 9th 1863, Grey issued a proclamation addressed to seven Maori tribes: "All persons of the native race living in this Manukau district, and the Waikato frontier, are hereby requested immediately to take the Oath of Allegiance to Her Majesty the Queen and to give up their arms to an officer appointed by Government for that purpose. Natives who comply with this order will be protected." On the same day, in reference to the news that the Maori Kingites were planning a bloodthirsty attack on Auckland, Grey also proclaimed that because it was impossible for the police and military at night time to distinguish between "friends and foes" "It is therefore required of all friendly disposed Maoris, that they abide within and not move about outside, lest they get into trouble. It has also been ordered that every Maori found on the streets of the town after dark, be apprehended." Two days later, on July 11th, Grey ordered the invasion of the Kingite territories.

END NOTES APPENDIX A

[1] The Treaty was first signed on February 6th 1840 by representatives of the British Crown and some Maori chieftains. It was aimed at deflecting Maori antagonism to the declaration of British sovereignty over New Zealand. Its initial aim was to give the Maori full rights as British subjects, while at the same time recognising the Maori ownership of their lands and forests.

[2] In total there were nine signed bilingual copies of the Treaty of Waitangi sent out to all the tribes. The English text and the Maori text differed, particularly in regard to the meaning of "having and ceding sovereignty". Indeed, the concept of "sovereignty" was alien and not understood by the Maoris, a matter which was to cause much trouble a decade later.

[3] Te Wherowhero of Waikato (who had not signed the Treaty of Waitangi) became the first Maori King in 1858.

APPENDIX B

An Overview of South Sea Islander legislation

Refs: *SUGAROPOLIS* Journeys to The Australian South Sea Islander: Story of the Gold Coast Region: http://www.goldcoast.qld.gov.au/documents/bf/history-south-sea-islanders-booklet.pdf

SUGAR SLAVES By Imelda Miller https://www.qhatlas.com.au/content/sugar-slaves

ON AUGUST 14th 1863 the schooner *Don Juan*, arrived in Moreton Bay. Aboard were 67 indentured labourers from the islands of Melanesia in the western part of the South Pacific. They had been engaged by Captain Robert Towns, a member of the New South Wales Legislative Assembly and businessman, to work on his 4,000 acre (1618 hectare) cotton plantation, *Townsvale*, on the Logan River, South Queensland.

The South Sea Island labourers, often called Kanakas in those days (now often regarded as a pejorative word), were mainly recruited from the Solomon Islands, the New Hebrides, Vanuatu, and New Caledonia, though others were taken from the Loyalty Islands. They had begun working in Queensland in the *beche de mer* industry in 1860 and had then, around 1863, found work on Robert Towns' cotton estate on the Logan River.

A series of parliamentary acts, both Queensland State, and later, Federal, were passed to deal with this South Sea Islander influx of labour. Despite early incidents of "blackbirding" or kidnapping workers from the Pacific area, the Queensland Government went to some lengths to legislate for fair treatment and pay for these labourers.

CRUCIAL DATES

1868: Polynesian Labourers Act and Pacific Labourers Act passed.

1869: the Queensland Government created a Select Committee on the operation of the Polynesian Labourers Act.

1872: Britain passed the Pacific Islanders Protection Act in a further attempt to manage the South Sea Islander labourers in Australia and Fiji.

1873: the Electoral Districts Act created the division of Logan, and Philip Henry Nind was elected its first representative. He was an advocate of South Sea Islanders and made efforts to improve their working conditions.

1880: the Queensland Government passed the Pacific Islanders labourers Act, the first major legislative revision since 1868.

1882-84: recruiting extended into the archipelago east of New Guinea.

1884: The Queensland Government passed an amendment to the 1880 Act to limit the employment of Australian South Sea Islanders (ASSI) to tropical agriculture but created an exemption category known as Ticket Holders who had arrived before September 1879 and were exempt from all further special legislation. There were 835 Ticket Holders in 1884, 716 in 1892, 704 in 1901 and 691 in 1906.

1884-5: the Queensland Government established a Royal Commission into Recruitment of Labour in New Guinea and Adjacent Islands. This led to Queensland ceasing labour recruiting in the archipelagos east of New Guinea and henceforth recruited only from islands now included in Vanuatu and the Solomon Islands.

1890: Queensland signalled the end of the labour tradeby 1890.

Queensland introduced an amendment to the 1880 Act to begin the Pacific Islanders' Fund, partly to distribute the wages of deceased ASSI.

1892: Queensland Premier Griffith announced the extension of the labour trade "for a definite but limited period of, say ten years". By then, almost 60,000 South Sea Islanders had been brought to Australia since 1863.

1901: under pressure from the Union movement which claimed the Kanakas were taking jobs from "white Australians", the newly-formed Commonwealth Government of Australia legislated for a 'White Australia Policy', including the Pacific Islanders Act which ordered the deportation of all ASSI.

By 1901: there were 9,327 Islanders in Australia, spread from Torres Strait to the Tweed District in Northern NSW and many of them did not want to go back to their island homes, leading to the formation in Mackay of The Pacific Islanders' Association to argue against deportation and to achieve better conditions for the Islanders.

1903 to 1905: eight petitions were presented to the Queensland and Commonwealth governments on behalf of Islanders due to be deported. In March, two hundred ASSI from Rockhampton petitioned the Governor of Queensland.

In September 3,000 Islanders signed a petition to King Edward VII.

The Commonwealth Government introduced the *Sugar Bounty Act* to subsidise sugar produced only with white labour.

1905: the Governor of Fiji agreed to take Queensland Islander deportees.

1906: a Queensland Royal Commission into the Sugar Industry recommended that certain categories of Islanders be allowed to remain in Australia.

1907-8: apart from the exempted categories, all remaining Islanders were deported. Around 2,000 remained and formed the nucleus of the present-day islander community.

1908: Britain and France established the New Hebrides Condominium. The Pacific Islanders Branch of the Queensland Immigration Department was closed.

1913: Queensland's Sugar Cultivation Act required non-Europeans to apply for certificates of exemption in order to be employed in any capacity in sugar growing. They were forced to take a reading and writing test with 50 words in any language as directed by the Inspector before they were allowed to grow or cultivate sugar cane in Queensland.

APPENDIX C

Cooper-Browne Genealogy

BECAUSE THOMASINE had so many children, and her children had so many children, this Appendix will deal only with the first and second generations – there is no space in this volume for more. However, family archivists Genevieve Grainger and Sue Mills have each diligently traced all the Cooper-Browne descendants to this day.

THE COOPERS

Thomasine and her first husband, Edward James Cooper, had five children:

Mary Thomasine; their eldest child, known as May, was born on April 25th 1856. She emigrated to Australia with Thomasine and Jack and married **Henry Schneider** on April 3rd 1879. Henry changed his surname by deed poll to Carlton during World War 1 because, despite his forebears for several generations having been British citizens, the name carried German connotations.
Henry Carlton passed away at *Umpinido*, their home in Nerang, on February 17th 1917 leaving his widow, May, and four daughters and a son:

Julia April 2nd 1880 – 1960);
Henry (March 27th 1882 – August 28th 1951);
Cecily Pearl April 24th 1885 – ?);
Katherine Una (January 20th 1892 – 1975);
Vivian Thomasine (September 9th 1895 – 1959)

Their son, Henry, sailed to England in 1917 and entered the war, returning to Nerang to resume his old profession of glass blowing, later striking out on his own account
The widowed May made her home in Brisbane with her two youngest daughters.
Their first daughter, Julia, and second daughter, Cecily, had lived in Brisbane for many years. Julia later became a nurse in Tasmania.

May sold the Nerang home to her nephew Edward J Cooper. May died on June 14th 1922.

Amelia (July 31st 1857 – March 31st 1861) was Thomasine and Edward James's second child. She died in England from Scarlet Fever, aged four.

Edward (August 25th 1858 – October 2nd 1916) was Thomasine and Edward James Cooper's third child. He was born at Garforth, Yorkshire on August 25th 1858. After emigrating to Australia, he spent his life at Nerang and was listed in the electoral roll as "Gentleman Farmer". He was also a leading figure in local politics and sporting events.

In 1881 Edward married Lena Hales aged 17 from Pontypool, Wales and had ten children:

Edward James (August 6th 1882 – August 5th 1927)
Ivy Lena (June 6th 1884 – July 15th 1905)
Amy Coral (December 27th 1885 – 1988)
Ethel Gladys (July 10th 1887 – July 24th 1982)
Herbert Hayles (May 20th 1889 – April 5th 1910)
Cecil Meredith (March 17th 1891 – November 1st 1980)
Thomasine Stella (January 27th 1893 – March 16th 1985)
Eva Octavia (February 21st 1895 – May 16th 1995)
Frank Wellington (June 18th 1897 – November 8th 1983)
Cherril Roberts (January 27th 1900 – August 1977)

Edward Cooper died on October 2nd 1916 aged 58 years. His untimely death was due to pneumonia caught while rescuing somebody from the river. Lena died in 1963 aged 102.

Roland Meredith Cooper was born on the 1st March 1860 at Hawes, Yorkshire. After emigrating to Australia with Thomasine and Jack, he grew up to marry Florence Eveline Augusta Tamlyn on April 18th 1906. They had four children:

Valma Florence (March 17th 1907 –)
Roland Tamlyn (March 29th 1909 – July 14th 1990)
Keith Meredith (July 5th 1911 – ?)
Colin Cherrill (November 27th 1913 – December 23rd 1997)

Herbert Cooper,"Bertie", was the youngest Cooper son. He was born on May 20th 1863, six weeks after his father died. After emigrating to Australia with Thomasine and Jack he grew up to marry Minnie Alberta Cecil Hardinge. They had two children:
Atholstan Edmund (May 20th 1901 – February 19 1960)
Viola May (November 23rd 19?? –)

Herbert was a partner with brother Roland in a fruit market in Brisbane. He died in 1932.

The Coopers had prize winning cattle (mostly Ayrshire) and the boys looked after the dairy.
In the 1920s or 1930s Roland and Herbert, "Bertie", sold their land to Edward's sons Frank Wellington and Cherrill Roberts. Roland and Bertie then went to live in Brisbane and had a fruit exchange at the Turbot St Markets, exporting some of their fruit to England. They are also listed as agents for a steamer owned by the Philpotts.

THE BROWNES
In total, Thomasine had 11 living children. From her second marriage, to Walter John "Jack" Browne. Thomasine had six living children plus two sets of twins who died at birth, and another, unnamed, baby whose death was possibly the result of a miscarriage.

Thomasine Anne – Thomasina or Ina as she was known, was Thomasine and Walter John "Jack" Browne's first child, born on May 9[th]1865. She married John George Brown in 1887. He was Deputy Registrar General of Queensland. They had two children, a daughter. **Clare**, and a son, **John.** Thomasine Anne was widowed in 1916 and never remarried. She died in Sydney in 1945.

Walter Alfred John was Thomasine and Jack's second child, born November 12th 1866. He is mentioned in various texts as either Jack or John. He married Annie Eliza Lancaster at St John's Church, Brisbane on June 1st 1898. John and Annie had two children:

Wilga Lancaster (1903 – ?)
Waverney Rosalind (1908 – ?)

A family disagreement saw Walter leave home and set up as an agent at Southport. Sadly, he was kicked by a horse and died a fortnight later from pneumonia leaving his wife and two young daughters.

Faith Eva Agnes was born on 6th August 1868. She married James Hoy and they had three children:

John James (1908 – ?)
Ruth Alice (1910 – 1996)
Evelyn Faith (1912 – 2000)

Faith and James Hoy lived lower down the Nerang River on the same side as Edward Cooper and Lionel Browne. James Hoy died on 29th May 1928 but Faith lived on until 28th April 1955 and died at the age of 86.

Ada Maude was born on 30th October 1872 and married William Godfrey Holden Rudd on June 18th 1902. He was the veteran Chairman of Nerang Shire Council, They had one son, **William Rudd** (1902 – 1963).

The Rudds lived and farmed at Mudgereeba. Ada's husband, William, died in1948 and Ada died on August 27th 1963, aged 91.

Lionel Edgar Browne, known as "Barney", was born on July 2nd 1876, and married Catherine Margaret Graham on January 16th 1907 and is believed to have been in the Moreton Regiment with his father at one stage.
Lionel and Catherine Margaret had a daughter, **Elma Knox** (1910 – ?) and a son, **Robert Edgar** (1907 – 1971).

The electoral roll of 1905 lists Lionel living and farming at *Ejuncum* with Thomasine, Rosamond and Faith. The roll of 1912 lists him still at *Ejuncum* with Thomasine and Catherine Margaret. Later, Lionel and Catherine Margaret moved to their own farm, *The Bamboos*, at Nerang,
Lionel and Catherine Margaret and their daughter, Elma, left Nerang in the 1920s. According to Elma it was a drought which finished Lionel's farming efforts. She said that the cows were breaking their legs in the cracks in the ground.
Moving to Brisbane did not improve Lionel's fortunes. He did gardening and odd jobs to make ends meet. Lionel and Catherine Margaret retired to the Chermside Garden Settlement, a facility now run by the Uniting Church. Lionel helped by milking the cows, but the management put a stop to this when a cow backed into him and broke his ribs when he was 80. After his wife's death Lionel was married again to an elderly spinster, Emma Packer. She predeceased Lionel, who died on December 31st 1959.

Rosamond Alice, the last child of Walter and Thomasine, was born on October 8th 1877 and was the first child to be baptised at St Margaret!s Anglican Church, Nerang, on January 20th 1878. Ros was engaged to a young man who came from The Disputed Plains in Northern NSW. Family lore relates that his sister became pregnant out of wedlock and the Browne family deemed the liaison unsuitable. Rosamond never married and subsequently became the companion of Captain Pollock's widow.

Rosamond worked first at the Taxation Department where she was employed for some years before she was transferred to the Department of Posts and Telegraphs as librarian of the Queensland Postal Institute, which position she held for 25 years. Trained as a horsewoman by her brother, Jack Browne, Rosamond won many prizes at local shows and was renowned for her prowess at high jumps, always riding side-saddle. She was also renowned for her happy personality and for producing a pair of pistols which she would fire at midnight at every New Year's Eve party.

Rosamond died on March 4th 1949.

Today most of the descendants of the Brownes and Coopers are scattered far and wide with few affiliations with Nerang. *Birribon*, which stood for over 100 years, was pulled down, and the land is now part of the Carrara Sports Complex. *Ejuncum* is now the Allambe Garden of Memories, and for many years a jacaranda and a palm tree existed on the site to indicate where the house stood.

BIBLIOGRAPHY

NEWSPAPERS AND PUBLICATIONS
NEW ZEALAND 1844 – 1863
AUSTRALIA 1862 – 1920

Brisbane Courier
Colonist, Vol V1, Issue 602, 31 July, 1862
Daily Southern Cross
Hawkes Bay Herald
New Zealander
New Zealand Herald
01 Newsletter Gold Coast Hinterland Heritage Museum Inc.
Queensland Times
The Queenslander
Rockhampton Bulletin and Central Queensland Advertiser
Telegraph (London)
The Illustrated London News
The Times, (London)
Tweed Daily News 1880 – 1921

BOOKS

Belich, James, *The Victorian Interpretation of Racial Conflict* (Montreal and Kingston, London, Buffalo. McGill-Queen's University Press1986)

Browne, Lyn, *The Two Families of Thomasine Browne.* (1941.) Unpublished manuscript courtesy Sue Mills. Now available online at: National Library Wellington, NZ under the title *The Two Families of Thomasine Meredith*

Cowan, James, *The New Zealand Wars: A History of the Maori Campaigns and the Pioneering Period, Volume 1 1845-64*, New Zealand, W. A. G. Skinner, government printer, 1923. (Also available online)

Dalton, B.J. *War and Politics in New Zealand 1855-1870.* (Sydney, Sydney University Press, 1967.)

Dictionary of National Biography. Volumes 1-22

Longhurst, Robert *Nerang Shire: A History To 1949.* (Queensland, The Albert Shire Council, 1994.)

BIBLIOGRAPHY

Peters, Ivo, *The Train Now Departing.* (UK, BBC Books, 1988.)

ONLINE REFERENCES

*A History of Last-Resort Lending and Other Support for Troubled Financial Institutions in Australia.
(https://www.rba.gov.au/publications/rdp/2001/2001-07/

ANCESTRY. www.ancestry.com.au

Brisbane Fire 8 pm Dec 1, 1864
https://en.wikipedia.org/wiki/Great_fire_of_Brisbane

Imelda Miller, *Sugar Slaves,*
https://www.qhatlas.com.au/content/sugar-slaves

Sugaropolis Journeys to The Australian South Sea Islander: Story of the Gold Coast Region
http://www.goldcoast.qld.gov.au/documents/bf/history-south-sea-islanders-booklet.pdf

WIKIPEDIA. www.wikipedia.org

DOCUMENTS

Australian Archaeology, No. 77, Preprint. Astronomical Orientations of Bora Ceremonial Grounds in Southeast Australia. Robert S. Fuller1,2, Duane W. Hamacher1,3 and Ray P. Norris1,2,4 1 Warawara Department of Indigenous Studies, Macquarie University, NSW.

Australian War Scares of the Nineteenth Century, Paper delivered in 1968 by Clem Lack, University of Queensland Library.

Brisbane's Water Supply: the Queen Street Fire of 1864. (By Charles Melton.) [Read at a meeting of the Historical Society of Queensland on September 1st 1924.]

Browne, Waverney, *Letters to Bundall*, Local Studies Library, Southport.

Thomasine

Cooper, Edward, unpublished Diaries, Local Studies Library, Southport

Cooper, Lena, unpublished Diaries, Local Studies Library, Southport

Cooper, Lena, unpublished Manuscript, Local Studies Library Southport.

England and Wales National Probate Calendar 1808 – 1966
German Missionaries in Australia, a web-directory of international encounters. By Regina Ganter. Griffith University

Letters, Wills and other family documents, courtesy Sue Mills.

Nerang Divisional Board. Nerang Shire Council Valuation Register Rate Book. Microfilm 1880 – 1949

Nerang Divisional Board. Nerang Shire Council. Minutes March 1893

New Zealand Gazette October 20th 1864, published in the *Timaru Herald*, vol 1, issue 23, November 12th 1864

Papers of Sir William Keith Ball, National Archives, UK.

Queensland Immigration and the Black Ball Line by Warwick Foote, read at a Meeting of the Royal Historical Society of Queensland on February 23rd 1978

*Reserve Bank of Australia RDP 2001-07: *A History of Last-Resort Lending and Other Support for Troubled Financial Institutions in Australia*
http://www.goldcoaststories.com.au/nerang-river/

Results of Rainfall Observations made in Queensland, H.A. Hunt, Commonwealth Meteorologist, 1914.
http://www.bom.gov.au/qld/flood/fld

Richard Edward's Will, courtesy Herefordshire Archive and Records Centre

UK Railway Employment Records, 1833 – 1956

www.ingramcontent.com/pod-product-compliance
Lightning Source LLC
Chambersburg PA
CBHW071237250626
47163CB00001B/226